The Chirping Cricket Desires the Ripened Crop

Kon Blacke

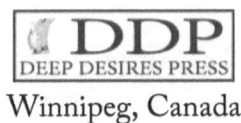

DEEP DESIRES PRESS

Winnipeg, Canada

Developmental editor Francisco Feliciano
Proofreader: Margaret Larson

Published July 2023 by Deep Desires Press, an imprint of Story Perfect Inc.

Deep Desires Press
PO Box 51053 Tyndall Park
Winnipeg, Manitoba R2X 3B0
Canada

Visit http://www.deepdesirespress.com for more scorching hot erotica and erotic romance.

Subscribe to our email newsletter to get notified of all our hot new releases, sales, and giveaways! Visit deepdesirespress.com/newsletter to sign up today!

The Chirping Cricket
Desires the Ripened Crop

The First Day

1.1: Boy agrees to be his Master's sexual submissive and houseboy. He must seek permission for any activities he desires to do that don't involve Master, other than work duties or commitments to family and friends.

Monday, 8:00 am

Eli Shigeru, making sure he didn't step on any of the joins between the tiling of the convenience store's floor, counted in his head the paces needed to get to his goal, pay, then get out.

It should be no more than forty-eight steps…he hoped.

He also moved quietly and quickly, not wanting to bring about any unnecessary attention on himself. He didn't want any delays or extra steps while avoiding people who could, *who would*, hinder him either. As such, he already had his wallet in hand to help with preventing any unnecessary delays.

Wherever he went, be it in a convenience store or a bookshop, he never tried to make himself known unless he had to. Never ever. He liked blending in with the background. Preferred it that way because of what had happened to him when he was a teenager.

At the moment, he didn't want to think about his

past; that already haunted him enough. No, his priority now was to get what he came for so he could get out of the store and go to work. As such, he quickly reached into the refrigerated cabinet to grab the carton of milk he needed: a litre of A2 low fat for his sensitive stomach.

Turning, twenty-two paces done, he was relieved to see the coast was clear to the cashier. A reason why Eli came so early was to avoid the crowds. It also lessened the chances of anyone recognizing him—the less people who knew he was here, the better.

Once he'd paid for the milk, he left the store; the forty-eight paces were done, a relief for sure. He now headed for the flower shop—a minefield of joins in paving, cracks in concrete and roads, and other obstacles that always set him on edge. Obstacles like having to touch the 'walk' button at the two pedestrian crossings between the convenience store and the flower shop amongst many of them.

Work was four hundred paces away. To make matters worse, there were a lot of people around already. Eli sucked in a deep breath, steeling his resolve to push himself to build up the courage so he could head toward his next goal.

Mason, his manager and best friend, would be waiting for him there. Waiting for the milk, too, for their morning coffees. Coffees they always shared before getting on with the day.

Eli loved Mason, his best friend for life, no doubt.

When Eli arrived at work, dodging any passers-by and other obstacles because he kept close to the buildings, of course Mason was waiting for him. What's more, as soon as Eli was seen, his friend opened his arms so they could become wrapped in each other's embrace.

For now, Eli felt safe and sound.

"You're a little late this morning," Mason said lightly once they parted, taking the carton of milk off Eli.

Eli felt his cheeks burn. "Sorry...the owner of the convenience store wanted to have a longer chat than his usual *good morning, how are you?*"

Mason giggled. "Don't apologize. It's all good."

Eli felt better, but then something struck him; his mind never giving him a moment of peace even when things were good, like now. "Did you talk to your Uncle Joe?"

Mason nodded. "I did."

"Well...?"

Mason offered a cute smile, but one that held nerves if Eli was reading him correctly—which he usually did. "I think we'll talk about it once we've had our coffee and started today's orders, okay?" A pause from his friend as the shop's front door was unlocked, lights turned on, and the open sign placed face out to the street.

They drank their coffee in relative silence.

Soon, the day began in earnest, the first few customers arriving. It was a good thing Mason dealt with all of them. He was a natural at it anyway, always smiling and pleasant. Eli's job was the ordering, arranging, and delivery of the flowers. He could cope with that, mostly thanks to Mason and his support.

His best friend was the only one who understood him.

After sixty-two minutes, excruciatingly long as far as Eli was concerned while he prepared a bunch of white lilies for a funeral, the flowers to be picked up by the courier driver before lunch, he asked, "What did he say? Your uncle, I mean?"

Mason, seeing off a customer with a cheery goodbye, turned to Eli. "I wondered how long you'd last before you asked me again."

"Well...stop teasing me." Eli had finished the flowers for the funeral, already preparing the next order: a bunch of Chrysanthemum's for an elderly lady's birthday that'd been ordered by her grandson. "What did he say?"

"He said he's found a friend of a friend who can help you."

Eli's eyes widened and he felt his heart beat harder all of a sudden, almost making him giddy. "Someone who can get my brother back from that gangster Yukkon?"

"Yeah, from what I understand."

But Eli then felt a stab of nerves. "What...happens next? When will he come see me? I mean, can I even contact this man? Or will he contact me? Will he want to be paid? I can't afford too much, you know—"

Mason looked at him, doing his best "please calm down" face Eli knew was a common expression. "I made sure to tell Uncle Joe to organize it so that he'd contact you, so you don't have to worry about that."

"When?" Eli dropped the floral scissors he was holding, the metal clanking on the benchtop. "Today? And where? Here? Or somewhere else?"

Mason shook his head. "It's been arranged for him to

come here during your lunch break today—I hope you don't mind?"

Eli blinked. Of course, he didn't mind. This man, this stranger, he could be the one who helped rescue Jiro from a fate he didn't want to even think about.

After a moment, counting the seconds in his head, almost one hundred twenty of them as he calmed, hope rising within him most of all, he replied, "Can I have a longer lunch break today, then? I don't want to have to rush eating because I've been talking to someone. My digestion is a mess…worse since Jiro was kidnapped."

Mason put his hand upon Eli's shoulder. "We're all worrying about Jiro. But just so you know, the man Uncle Joe organized through his associates said he'll bring you lunch. His treat. He used to own a restaurant or something, from what I heard."

Eli wasn't sure about eating food he hadn't seen before he agreed to eat it, but accepted what Mason had said to him. What choice did he have? And at least *something* was finally happening after almost a week since the note and severed finger had been delivered to him with no further instructions since.

Which he found strange.

Didn't people like Yukkon, evil men like him anyway, make their demands immediately? Especially if they were holding a hostage…right? Wasn't that how it usually worked?

In any case, Eli couldn't worry about such things just yet. He had enough on his plate already. His lunch with a stranger now the biggest one of all.

Monday, 12:30 pm

Eli sat, one leg jiggling nervously, stomach turning painfully, in the flower shop's lunch room at the table he always had. The one with the best view of the staff room's door. He couldn't have his back to an entrance. No way.

It was 12:31 pm now. The man was sixty seconds late. Not good.

Not a great first impression, either.

Then, just as he was about to call Mason, the door creaked opened. The man entered silently. Eli's throat tightened as their eyes met, the dark pools of enigmatic wonder he couldn't help but stare at.

This was it.

Eli swallowed.

The man sat opposite Eli without invitation, holding a smile even more mysterious than his eyes. And even though Eli noted he was short in stature, handsome in a rugged sort of way complete with a dainty golden septum ring and the lines of his life all over his face—especially around his eyes—his long, black hair was tied up in a neat ponytail making him seem refined at the same time. A strange dichotomy, Eli mused.

He was also older than Eli, perhaps by ten years...maybe more.

Eli swallowed again, more audible that time.

Under the man's hawk-like scrutiny, as if Eli were a mouse...or so it seemed...Eli found the courage within him to say, "I'm Eli Shigeru...and I believe you can help me, sir?"

A shift of weight. "My name is Kane." He extended out his hand.

Eli looked at it for the longest time, noting how the man hadn't offered his surname. "Um…I don't shake people's hands."

"I see." Kane withdrew his gesture. "Then how do you greet someone you first meet?"

"I try to avoid doing it."

"My, my, that must be a very lonely life, you lead."

Eli didn't like the track of this conversation for 12.37 in the afternoon and without having eaten. "Can you help me or not?"

Another shift of weight. "Blunt and to the point. I like that." Kane folded his arms, leaning back in his chair. "I can rescue your brother Jiro from Yukkon for fifty-thousand dollars, and th…"

Eli didn't hear the rest because he'd almost fallen off his chair in shock; the legs of it scraping loudly against the wooden flooring as he moved back suddenly.

"I can't afford that!" he blurted when he'd composed himself enough.

Kane looked Eli up and down, holding his smile that seemed to have turned wolfish all of a sudden. "Then perhaps we can come to some other arrangement, Eli Shigeru?"

Eli then felt the weight of Kane's stare. That, and the warmth of his cheeks, right down to his neck, at the same time. "What sort of arrangement?"

From within a brown paper bag, something Eli only just then noticed Kane had carried in with him because the man's presence pervaded all else, overtook his senses, he produced two banana leaf-wrapped packages from a large clear plastic takeaway container. On opening it, the lid being pulled away made that annoying cracking noise they always did.

Kane asked, "Perhaps we can share the meal I prepared before we get down to the proper business of things, hmm?"

Eli, feeling giddy now, nodded. "What did you make?"

Kane expertly opened the banana leaves after placing one onto a plate for Eli, the other for himself. "They are kibi dango—rice dumplings."

Eli knew what they were, not needing the clarification but appreciating it anyway, replied, "Oh, I love those—are they sweet?"

"They are."

Eli realized how hungry he was as soon as he feasted his eyes on what was presented for him, six perfectly rounded and brilliant white rice dumplings, large ones too. They would certainly fill him up.

"Thank you, sir." He accepted the kibi dango eagerly.

For the next twelve minutes they ate in silence.

During that time, Eli relaxed enough to enjoy the lunch prepared for him. It was tasty. Just right with the perfect balance of chewiness and bounce after each bite. And much to his surprise, he also relaxed enough to enjoy Kane's company, even if only a little.

He also managed a smile.

The man named Kane moved delicately, he noted.

Carefully too. As though each gesture and expression were measured. Eli knew how that felt, that was him every day of his life since high school.

When they'd eaten, Kane cleaned up and sat back down.

It was then Eli's impatience got the better of him, his anxiety too. "I think it's time for you to tell me what you have in mind."

Kane leaned forward. "You are a very handsome young man, Eli."

At that, Eli was taken aback. "I…thanks. But what has *that* got to do with anything?"

"My dear boy, it has a lot to do with everything."

Eli, even more stunned, managed, "What are you trying to say, sir?"

Kane moved his hand so that his long fingers brushed over Eli's knuckles, as a lover would do to show affection. A little jolt shot through Eli at that touch, but it mostly made him suck in a breath and fight the urge to withdraw.

In fact, Eli had to fight everything within him not do so, much to his regret. After all, and as much as it came down to this, Kane really was the only man who could help him get Jiro back from that monster Yukkon safely. The *only* man.

"I think we can come to another arrangement, if you're willing."

Eli didn't need an interpreter to understand what Kane meant by that. But even so, he glanced at the door. Eight paces. That's how many it would take to get out of the staffroom. Another ten and he could be back with

Mason on the shop's selling floor. He could get a hug from his friend then.

Be in his safe place.

But Eli, for the sake of his brother, steeled himself. "I suppose you want me to suck your dick, then…right?"

Kane laughed. "Oh, you're adorable if you think that would be worth the cost of my fee no matter how good you think you are at it."

Eli was dumbfounded. "Then what is it you want from me, sir?"

From Kane's jacket, embroidered beautifully with a traditional Japanese stylized dragon, golden sleeved too, he produced an envelope. He pushed it across the table.

"Open it," he ordered. "Once you've read what it requires you to do for me because you can't pay me, please sign it if you want to see Jiro alive again." With a fluid motion, a flourish of his wrist, he also produced a pen, handing it to Eli after clicking on the end of it.

Eli studied the man. "And if I don't sign?" he asked, picking up the paper then taking the pen, hands trembling as he felt more and more like the mouse here than earlier.

"It's entirely up to you, naturally." A smile more knowing, less wolfish too. "But I know Yukkon. At the moment he's amused by your brother. But when he's not…my, my, that's when the bodies start piling up. Trust me, I know this as the truth, Eli."

Eli's heart pounded, fearing the worst.

He opened the envelope, paper shaking as much as he was. What he read almost made him faint. He needed a moment as his vision went blurry, the words on the pages more so, and his heart skipped beats. Eli had to gulp great breaths, trying to get oxygen back into his lungs, making sure to breathe deeper from his stomach like his therapist had taught him.

What he held was a Dom/sub contract.

A contract of eleven pages outlining in detail what Eli would be required to do. What he *had* to do. He was to become a submissive to Kane in all things, including giving him sex whenever he desired it.

"I...can't sign this..." Eli mumbled once he'd glanced over most of it, paragraphs and paragraphs of information, from how he was to be trained and what was expected of him during and after that time, including how he was to groom himself, where he slept, and what he was allowed to eat.

Eli noted it was food only prepared by Kane.

"Then simply return the contract," Kane said, holding his hand out. "I'll then bid you farewell, Eli Shigeru, because I know you don't have fifty-thousand dollars, do you?" He looked around. "I don't know many flower shop workers who *could* pay that much money."

Eli felt as though he was sandwiched between a rock and a hard place. He couldn't pay. He also didn't want to sign the contract. But most of all, he wanted Jiro back with him, safe and sound.

He sighed in resignation. "How long do I have to be your submissive for?"

Kane's lips curled. "As it states right there in black and white, you'll be mine for one month, during which time you will live with me as well as meet my every desire."

"Why only a month?"

A press of lips now. "Because that's how long Jiro has before Yukkon slits his throat and sends you his head in a box."

Eli's heart raced, sweat forming on his brow as the room closed in around him, breathtakingly so as his fear for his brother gripped him as much as his own. "H-how do you…know this?"

"I just do," was all the man offered, as enigmatically as his first smile.

Eli glanced at the contract. "Then I have no choice here, do I?"

"There's always a choice, Eli." A pause, one carefully considered Eli imagined, before Kane added, "But just so you know, I won't even attempt a rescue of your brother until you've fulfilled your contract to me."

A million questions crashed into Eli's head, hurting him. "You've thought of everything, including the timing of all this, haven't you, Kane?"

A tilt of his head, a small but respectful bow really, from the man that time. "A businessman tries to consider all contingencies, yes."

Eli almost laughed; he would have if this wasn't so serious. "I won't please you, no matter what you believe. That much I know." He dated and signed the contract, *Elias Hirato Shigeru*, making sure every letter of his full name was clear and unmistakable.

Kane's expression brightened. "You please me already."

Eli harrumphed, thinking about how it was Kane who

would now be the one to experience what daily life was like for him; a complete mess, really. "Just so you know, I can't even look after myself—just ask Mason."

Kane stood, chair scraping against the wood. "Then perhaps it's time the burden of your care is given to someone else for a while so it doesn't worry you any longer."

He offered his hand once more. That time Eli took it, feeling Kane's warmth through their connection most of all. A strange thing, really.

"I can assure you that'll never happen."

"We shall see."

The Second Day

1.2: Boy must keep himself clean at all times. He must also keep his body and pubic hair trimmed to his Master's liking. Boy cannot get a haircut unless approved by his Master.

Tuesday, 9:00 am

According to the contract Eli had signed, he was given a day to pack what he'd need for the time he'd spend at Kane's house as his obedient submissive. Once more, nerves and his anxiety found him.

"What do I even pack if I'm going to be someone's sex slave?" he said to himself as he zipped up his suitcase, deciding to go light with his choices; T-shirts and shorts mostly, plus all the underwear he owned as well as his mountain of personal care products.

Then again, and with a turning stomach, he realized he probably wouldn't require much clothing...for obvious reasons.

How did it come to this?

But Eli knew all too well. He *had* to do whatever he could to save Jiro, including giving himself to Kane to pay for his services so that could happen.

Thirty days.

It was only thirty days.

Eli sucked in a deep breath. He was as ready as he'd ever be, he supposed. And as if to make it even more of a reality, Kane, as efficient as Eli had already come to expect, had even helped Mason with a replacement for him at work.

The guy who'd perform Eli's job was a tall, brown-haired and cute boy named Thomy who had big hands and a bigger smile. Eli liked him on first sight.

Mason seemed to like Thomy as well; the conversation between them breezy and carefree already.

Eli, needing to be in his safe place one last time before he left, dropped his suitcase and folded himself into Mason's open arms.

Tears welled in his eyes.

"You be careful, all right," Mason whispered into Eli's ear as they embraced for the fourth time, that one the last Eli would receive for a month and the most love-filled too.

Eli would miss his best friend so, so very much.

"Promise me with all your heart," Eli began, "that if I'm not back in thirty days, get that hunky fiancé of yours to bust Yukkon's ass for what he's done. You have my permission to do so."

"That's a deal."

Kane was waiting for Eli in his car parked out the front of the flower shop, a sleek black modern Mercedes, dark tinted windows and full of every luxury imaginable inside. It was a giddying experience to sit within it, Eli feeling out of place all of a sudden. He certainly didn't belong here.

"You look most handsome today, Eli," Kane said with a voice that dripped of honey and promise.

Eli secured his seatbelt. "Let's just get on with this, please."

Kane didn't reply, but there was a flash of something across his expression. Something Eli wasn't sure about.

No matter, he was certain he'd soon find out.

When the driver had placed Eli's suitcase into the boot, making sure Kane was satisfied with how things were proceeding, he drove off toward Eli's new life for the month.

Eli began counting the traffic light's as they passed by. When he was up to five sets, that's when he couldn't help get the feeling that this would be the last time that he'd see the shop or his old life.

The last time he'd see Mason too.

"I want you to wear this, Eli." Eli, saddened by his thoughts, turned from the city's views to see Kane holding what was unmistakably a leather collar, studded and with a loop for a chain to be attached. "Do you want me to put it on for you?"

Eli wasn't sure about how he was supposed to respond, because according to what he'd signed up for he was to not only please Kane but answer him respectfully and positively as well at all times.

His hesitation must have been noted. "If I give you a choice, you *can* choose," Kane offered. "It's only when I order you to do something that you must comply."

Eli blurted, "What if I can't comply...for whatever reason?"

"Then, as clearly stated in the contract, you must get down on your hands and knees and give me your reasons for not being able to do as I've asked," the man stated matter-of-factly. "I will then make my judgement from there as to whether or not I accept your reason. If I don't, you will be punished."

Eli sucked in a breath of surprise. "I thought you said you'd care for me?"

"Of course, I will." A smile. "Remember, you are a precious possession of mine now and I'll never hurt you. But at the same time, you must do as is expected of you as my submissive—discipline being a part of that."

Eli glanced at the collar Kane was still holding.

Swallowing his pride so soon already, he answered, "Then...um, I'd like you to fit me with my collar, Kane."

"Call me Master from now on—I deem that the most appropriate term for you to use when addressing and answering me. As I will now call you 'boy' for the same reasons."

Another swallow. "I...I would like it if you were to put on my...collar for me, Master."

"Good boy." Eli leaned over, his head almost in Kane's lap, the man fitted the collar, checking with Eli often that it was snug but not too tight. "You cannot tamper with your collar unless I tell you to."

"I understand."

Before Eli sat back up, the sensation of the leather collar around his neck a strange one already, Kane brushed his hand tenderly over Eli's hair seventeen times, humming a tune not recognized.

As he did so, the man whispered, "You *are* such a handsome, boy."

Eli, admitting to himself that he didn't mind such gentle attention, replied, "Thank you for your compliment, Master."

It was almost a moment between them.

And to emphasize that, Kane's touch never left Eli. "I want you to stay like this with your head in my lap until we get to your new home, boy."

"Yes, Master."

Eli was then caressed more gently, not just his hair but his face as well. It almost tickled. Although, even though Kane's contact was warm, there was also a noticeable tremble there. What was that about? Was something expected of Eli now?

He therefore had to ask, "What else did you want me to do for you at the moment, Master?"

"For now, enjoy my attention and the ride."

Kane's touch continued.

With relief, Eli began to relax and feel…not safe…but not in danger either. That was strange in itself considering what was happening. How his thoughts had taken him down a path where he imagined he'd already have been required to perform a sexual act on Kane. Give him a blowjob.

Kane added, "As soon as we arrive, your training will begin, boy."

Eli's moment of peace didn't last long then. His anxiety and stress grew and grew within him, painfully so.

He had a fair idea what "training" meant.

In a brief but terrible moment of clarity, panic rose within Jiro as he heard a door shut. He was helpless. Not only was he bound and chained and left in the dark, he was naked too. Defenceless and unable to prevent what would happen to him. And he knew something horrible would happen to him soon.

His abuser had returned.

Tuesday, 10:32 am
Kane's home was like him, a dichotomy of absolutes. On the one hand, it was palatial with ornamental gardens, as large as any house Eli had ever seen in his life. On the other, and inside it, the place was cram-packed with luxurious furniture, books of all types, expensive looking ornaments, and everything else imaginable that could go into a house. There was even a life-sized taxidermized grizzly bear in the front living room.

Eli certainly felt out of place here, which didn't help his anxiety. In fact, because of that, he'd already counted the paces to the carpeted front room he found himself in from the entrance door.

There were eighteen.

Knowing that, he felt a teeny bit better; because if there was one thing he'd learned since high school, knowing the escape route and how quickly he could traverse it was a much-needed comfort.

Kane carried Eli's suitcase after dismissing the driver,

placing it down by the door. "I hope you like your new home, boy."

Eli wasn't sure, but replied, "I do..." And then because of himself, the spiralling thoughts he was immersed in because of being in unfamiliar surroundings, remembered to add "Master" before Kane no doubt chastised him for not offering the correct means of address.

Kane smiled, adding a nod; Eli was relieved by that sight.

Although, what the man said next chased away that relief quicker than if a manifestation of his past had appeared before him. "I want to inspect you properly now, boy."

The man stepped closer.

With everything Eli had in him, to every fibre of his being, he resisted the urge to step away or complete those eighteen paces to the front door, almost flinching, too, but proud of himself he hadn't. "What...do y-you mean...Master?" His heart raced though.

Kane, obviously noticing Eli blink in response to his proximity, nodded once more, clearly in understanding. He sat in the nearest chair, a soft comfortable recliner he sank into.

"You don't have to be shy around me, boy," he said. "Nothing will happen to you here that will hurt you, I promise. So why don't you take off your clothes for me? I'd love to see you naked."

And even though the man's voice was gentle and somewhat reassuring, there was no doubt Eli had to obey him, the intensity in his eyes more than enough evidence of that.

Eli gulped. "Yes, Master."

As he nervously slipped off his T-shirt, Kane made himself even more comfortable, leaning back, crossing one leg over the other before placing his hand upon his chin just so to show his complete and utter interest in what Eli was doing for him.

"My, my, you've got such a lovely smooth body, boy," Kane observed once the T-shirt was shed and Eli had begun thumbing at the button of his skinny fit chino pants, fingers trembling as he tried to undo it. "Cute little pink nipples, too. So very nice."

"Thank you, Master," Eli replied in the correct way.

Soon, he was down to his boxer briefs, his favorite blue pair, feeling exposed and vulnerable standing there under such scrutiny. He'd not been naked in front of anyone before. He'd never had a boyfriend. Hadn't even been kissed by a boy, either. Now everything was going to happen at once, he knew it; Eli not only agreeing to give himself willingly to Kane, but also give the man his virginity as well.

Eli hesitated as he thought about that. Again, he had to stop himself from dashing to the door against his better nature. The only thing that kept him under Kane's scrutiny, so out of his comfort zone, was his belief that Jiro would be saved because of what he did. He realized that thought was a noble one, even if it made his anxiety skyrocket.

"You seem very nervous," Kane observed.

Eli nodded. "It's…I'm okay."

Kane sat up. "Are you sure?"

Eli was surprised by the amount of consideration in the man's voice, more so than when they were in the car while he was being caressed as if he was a precious pet. As such, and steeling his resolve, he tugged down his underwear to reveal himself fully for his Master.

Kane sucked in a breath, eyes widening. "By the gods, you truly *are* a cute little thing, aren't you, boy?"

Eli's cheeks burned and he hung his head, looking down at himself now so exposed. "I'm sorry I'm not…I know you're disappointed by what I've got, because saying I'm cute…well—"

"Come here," Kane interrupted.

Eli felt his throat tighten. "Yes, Master."

Stepping out of his boxer briefs that'd fallen down to his ankles, Eli felt a chill course right through him, and not because of the cold, either. When he was within arm's reach of the man, Kane's expression softened. He then reached for Eli in an inviting way, open armed and open faced, one that held that lovely enigmatic smile just for him.

"Come and sit on my lap…please," Kane purred.

Eli did so, stomach turning, feeling ashamed and unable to look at Kane directly. "I'm sorry," he repeated.

Kane ran his gentle, almost methodical, but certainly caring touch, over Eli's leg closest to him, something which strangely reassured even though it moved inch by inch toward his exposed genitals. "Never apologize for who you are, my beautiful, handsome, and precious boy."

Stunned by his words spoken so softly, Eli then looked at Kane, seeing the conviction in his dark, mysterious eyes. "Even...even though I'm c-certainly not what you expected...or wanted, now that you've seen me n-naked?"

"You are perfect to me. Simply perfect, boy."

"W-what...?"

Before another word was spoken between them, Eli was brought into an embrace. He inhaled sharply because of its strength, the feels he got from their connection.

Being hugged had always been Eli's weakness.

To make it even more intense, for the longest time Eli was held with warmth encircling him, making him giddy. He liked it. A lot. To add to that, Kane's hands then moved tenderly all over and across Eli's exposed back with what he could only describe as something greater than affection.

Could it be love?

Not that he'd experienced love before.

Even so, the embrace resulted in a strange feeling finding Eli. One he couldn't quantify. How could he? And to experience anything like that from someone other than Mason, that was profound.

Very profound.

At that, Eli forgot his state of undress as his mind wheeled back to the times that he'd found himself within his safe place. Within Mason's arms, mostly. The place where all the ghosts of his past became vanquished, even if only for a little while. Where the memories of his homophobic bullies who'd cornered him within the boys' toilets that fateful day to beat the living crap out of him were also pushed aside.

Eli began to weep, softly at first.

As he fell deeper and deeper into himself while in Kane's arms, he could then feel each and every strike upon his flesh, fist and foot, as if they were being delivered right now. Eli soon let it all go. He cried like the floodgates had been opened, also wincing as he sucked in short sharp breaths in memory. He wanted to hide even more from it all, moving to do so in Kane's hold.

Kane held him tighter in response.

After that, Eli soon found he was blubbering uncontrollably, wetting Kane's shirt with his tears and the hate he felt toward himself because he was so weak that day and every single one since then.

It was the reason why the counting habit of his began. He had to know from that day onward how he could escape from a place if he found himself trapped, know without doubt how many steps he needed until he was free.

Free from all the hate.

Eli let it all out, every staining memory. He knew he also got his phobia about the joins between certain types of flooring from then as well. The toilet floor he was left bloody and beaten on was covered in tiles, tiny little squares, pristine and perfectly white. His blood had no trouble re-grouting those joins with his weakness beaten out of him.

A sight he'd never forget.

Eli cried and cried.

"Cry as long as you need to, my heart," Kane whispered. "I'm here for you."

Eli realized Kane hadn't called him "boy" that time. Had his outpouring of emotion changed their dynamic already? He wasn't sure. But no matter, Kane held him and held him until he was ready to resurface, face the world again. Face his demons that were never far away. Not ever.

When he finally sat up after what seemed forever, Kane, and without delay, quickly kissed the tears from off Eli's emotion-soaked face. "W-what was...that f-for... Master?" Eli was dumbfounded anyone would do that.

Kane ran his hands over Eli's legs again, his touch seemingly even more tender than before, if that was possible. "Let me show you just how beautiful and perfect you are."

Eli then got it. The reason the man had been so accommodating. He swallowed...hard. "You only accept me b-because you want to fuck me now, am I r-right?"

"No, you're not right." Kane's touch didn't falter. "And no, even though it is my right to do so, I'm not going to fuck you, boy. Not yet."

Okay, Eli couldn't believe that he'd be taken aback so many times in one day already. "Then w-what are you going to do to...me, Master?"

Kane replied, "I'm going to show you how to look after yourself before anything else happens."

Eli once more blushed.

"I try to look after myself, Master," he said, believing Kane must have smelled his musk oozing out of every pore while his emotions became dredged up like dark sticky oil engulfing a thriving ocean with its poison. "I shower every day."

"I meant by the way you present yourself." Kane gestured for Eli to get up. He did so, once more feeling the weight of the man's attention upon him. "I want you to keep your body hair trimmed from now on. Keep it nice and short, including your thick bush of pubic hair that's grown out of control there."

Eli felt his throat tighten as he looked down at himself. He was greeted by his, frightened as he was, little dick, smaller than usual he thought, all foreskin and not much else really.

"Even if I trim my pubes, which I will do so for you, Master, it won't make my dick any bigger, will it?"

Kane knitted his fingers, placing them to his chin, as if in thought again. "Did it occur to you that the smaller dicks are the better ones to suck on, boy?"

More surprise. "It didn't, no, Master."

"Tell me, how big does your cock get when you're fully erect, boy? And don't say you don't know; every boy knows the size of his own equipment, flaccid *and* hard."

Eli tried not to get even more embarrassed, but failed. "It's…four and a half inches…that's all."

"That's perfect."

Eli once more became surprised, a rare thing especially when it came to discussing things about himself. "Are you…sure?"

"I am." Kane sat up. "Now go trim your body hair as I've instructed. I want you to then shower—the bathroom is down the hall to the right, second door on the left. You'll find body hair clippers in the cabinet."

"Yes, Master."

"If I'm not here when you get back, don't worry, boy. I have an errand to run and won't be long, I promise. But remember, I want you to remain naked for me while inside the house and within the private gardens." That answered Eli's suitcase packing problem he'd had earlier. He didn't need clothing at all. "That way you will become so used to yourself in your natural state it will hopefully no longer cause you any stress. Do you understand, boy?"

Yes, I do, Master." Before Eli turned to go do as asked, he added, "Am I to clean myself...*everywhere?*"

"Just complete your usual cleaning routine for me for now, please."

"Then...you're really *not* going to fuck me?"

"One step at a time, boy. I want to understand you more before you give yourself completely to me. All right?"

"Thank you, Master."

Eli smiled.

Kane returned it, softer and with an even greater understanding, if Eli wasn't mistaken. "It's not how you imagined it would be, being my submissive, is it?"

"It's not, no. Not what I expected at all."

"What did you expect, then?"

"Not this." And that was as honest an answer as Eli could give.

The door to Jiro's cell opened, light flooding into the small room for a moment to blind him, his only option to turn away before it hurt his eyes too much.

As he heard his abuser's footsteps come closer, fear clawed at him, and he instinctively tried to get away. He couldn't. He was chained, he remembered. The rattle of it to remind him more than enough evidence of that fact. Helpless and hopeless, he had no choice but to accept whatever happened next.

His fear focused into hate.

Jiro didn't know how long he'd been left alone this time. An hour? A day? Two days? Time was meaningless when he was kept captive and drugged by an abuser who sexually assaulted him for pleasure whenever the urge struck the man.

"I see you're awake," his abuser said, voice honey-sweet as he sat on the bed Jiro was lying on and chained to; a squeak of springs and rattle of metal the result.

Jiro's skin crawled.

"Go fuck yourself, prick," he spat with a rasp, only thinking of vitriol to spit at the man.

What else could he do?

"So fiery today, aren't you? I like it. It turns me on even more."

Panic and repulsion in equal measure soon found Jiro as his abuser positioned himself between Jiro's legs. He knew he couldn't fight him off, either. Not even kick him. The drugs weakened him so much, made him nauseous if he moved too quickly, too.

They also gave him a massive headache.

"*Please* no," Jiro then pleaded as his hate quickly turned to fear again, knowing what would happen next.

He felt his abuser's cold lips kiss his dick; his skin crawling there to almost become painful. "You have such a lovely big cock. Have I told you that?"

"Fff...fuck o-off."

"Well, you do. You must be proud of it." Another kiss, that time on Jiro's foreskin along with a lick of the man's tongue. More repulsive shivers resulted. "You're so tasty too. And my, my, you've leaked a lot of pre-cum, haven't you? Does the thought of me raping you excite you, hmm?"

Jiro had to force his emotions down, swallowing them. He didn't want to cry in front of such a monster. Didn't want to give the man that satisfaction, either. "Just do what you came here to do and leave me alone."

"Are you giving me your permission? Oh, how very naïve of you to think I need it. Very naïve."

"Please...just leave me alone."

"That, I can't do. I've built up a bit of tension lately, and I need you to help me relieve it. Understand?"

"Get f-fucked."

The Third Day

1.3: Boy can only eat and drink in Master's presence unless explicit permission from Master is given for him not to do so. Boy will only consume food prepared by Master. Boy will also ask for permission before eating any food or drinking any drink.

Wednesday, 6:45 am

Eli woke in a strange bed, momentarily disorientated. An instant of panic followed. He sat up, slowly calming and gaining his bearings as the confused haze caused by his waking dissipated. He felt better on remembering. On seeing Kane peacefully asleep next to him.

He then stretched, feeling the invigoration of a new day overtake him; the sensation of harboring his morning erection found him too. Although at that, Eli then realized he was naked. He never slept with nothing on; he always wore boxer briefs at the very least. He remembered it'd taken him ages to get to sleep because of it, believing he'd squash his balls or something if he got into a weird position during the night. He just felt like everything down there was left unsecured without his underwear on.

That *would* take some getting used to.

Eli also discovered the sensation of the sheets against his exposed buttocks and genitals a strange one too, even if they were fancy Egyptian cotton-type ones. A high thread count, no doubt.

In fact, now that he thought about it, it'd also taken him a long time to get used to someone else being in bed with him. He'd never slept with anyone before. Not ever. And every movement Kane made, no matter how small, disturbed him. Even his breathing seemed loud within the silent blanket of night that pervaded Kane's house like a spectre wandering through a great hall.

But now it was morning, his first "real" day as a submissive. Although, and to be honest, Eli had absolutely no idea what to do. He had a month off work, paid for by Kane. So, did he just wait for his Master to wake up to tell him what to do? Did he stay in bed? Was he allowed out of the bed if Kane remained asleep? Or was Eli to wake him?

The contract he'd signed wasn't too clear on that; it only stated that he had to make himself available to Kane at all times, do as he was told unless there was a good reason for him not to. Was his Master being asleep a good reason?

Eli, through no fault of his own, began to get anxious. He didn't like when boundaries became blurred. At least that got rid of his erection. It was then a new sensation overtook him. Another common one.

As if reading his thoughts, Kane sleepily said, "You may go to the toilet, boy."

"Thank you, Master."

Eli pulled the bedclothing off himself, hopped out of bed, then dashed to the toilet within the ensuite that was only seven paces away from the bed. When there, he quickly did his business, ensuring to pull back his foreskin enough so as to prevent any build-up of urine underneath it before he got the chance to shower. Relieved, he washed his hands before returning to the bed Kane remained within.

"Did you sleep well, boy?" Kane asked, sitting up.

He was wearing exquisite pyjamas made of silk and embroidered with patterns of dragons and other creatures of Japanese folklore. So beautiful. The clothing suited him. Traditional but at the same time garish—two worlds together, as he was.

Eli, knowing he couldn't lie, replied, "I didn't...no, Master."

"You will get used to things."

"I hope so." Eli crawled back into bed, moving so he could hold Kane, not really knowing why but believing it was expected of him. "What can I do for you, Master?"

His actions and words must have pleased the man. "You are taking to your role quite nicely, aren't you?" A smile was beamed to emphasize his pleasure.

"I'm trying to do my best."

"It's good that you are." Kane kissed Eli's forehead. "Today, I want to begin your training so you can do for me what I truly desire."

From the way Kane said that, he got a feeling the man didn't quite mean he wanted to fuck Eli. That Kane desired something else. Then again...it could just be his overthinking. His anxiety too.

Eli replied, "I *think* I understand."

"You will fully understand soon." Kane offered one more kiss upon Eli's brow, tender and warm, before adding, "Now go take a shower while I prepare your breakfast, boy. I'm making eggs with furikake and a side of pickled vegetables for you this morning."

"That sounds delicious, thank you, Master."

And it did. Eli liked eggs poached with a seaweed, bonito, anchovy, and dried shrimp seasoning; he also liked picked vegetables, particularly the radish-like root vegetable known as daikon. But yet again, he wasn't sure of what was required of him.

Eli had to add, "Did you need me to clean myself more appropriately for you this time, Master?"

"Please, just make sure there isn't any smegma underneath your foreskin. For what I have in mind, your cock needs to be really clean. That's all I require from you for the moment."

Eli was really at a loss. "I um...I don't understand."

Kane smiled enigmatically. "Your training will begin with the food I make for you each day. As such, it will be high in protein and rich in foods that will make you taste sweeter."

Eli was almost in a constant state of surprise, truly. "You're talking about...the taste of my cum, right?"

Kane nodded. "When I'm satisfied you have the right taste after I've milked you, then we can proceed with the training of your anus for what I plan to use it for, my boy."

Eli certainly didn't know how to reply to that. Other than sticking his dick into Eli's ass, what other use for it could the man be talking about? Because yes, and by how their conversation had unfolded, Eli got the distinct feeling Kane wasn't discussing anal sex here.

Then what was he talking about?

His mind boggled, worryingly so. For Eli, anyway. He was simply dumbfounded as he tried to wrestle with the possibilities. And it was only 7:16 in the morning.

What a day already.

"Yes, Master," was all he managed as he pulled himself out of his spiralling.

Wednesday, 9:00 am

After he'd showered, ensuring he was cleaned as ordered, Eli was to call for Kane. He knew he wasn't to open any doors unless opened for him by his Master or he'd been given permission to do so.

Eli wasn't given such permission to open the bedroom's door.

He was therefore left with no choice. He didn't want to be punished for any disobedience. Because, as he could only imagine, no doubt any form of discipline would require being hit by something, either by a hand, cane, crop, or paddle across his bare buttocks. He'd seen such things in the bedside drawers, no mistaking what they were for. A sight that struck him with a terrible fear.

Eli couldn't be hit.

Not at all.

It would be too triggering, he knew. And from there, he wouldn't know how he'd cope. It could break him. Even more than he already was.

"I'm ready, Master!" he called.

Within moments, Kane entered. The man was carrying a tray full of the food he'd promised, freshly cooked and expertly so. It smelled divine too. Eli's stomach rumbled to emphasize not only that but the sudden hunger he felt.

"I think it would be lovely if we ate breakfast in my private garden this morning." Kane gestured with a tilt of his head toward the French doors framed by pristine white voile, soft and sheer, that dominated one wall of the bedroom. "You have my consent to open those doors, boy."

Eli did so.

They were soon in a most beautiful place. A place full of greenery and flowers in abundance, the scents of them both intoxicating and wonderful. Eli smelt jasmine most of all, but there were so many others. He loved it.

In the middle of the garden, there was a café style table and chairs sitting comfortably on a pristinely manicured lawn. Beyond that, an outdoor day bed, a comfortable scattering of cushions all over it.

"Sit, boy," Kane commanded.

"Yes, Master," Eli said obeying, thankful the seat he chose also had a cushion on it; he could only imagine how the wicker of the chair wouldn't be too comfortable against his buttocks and balls after a while without it.

From there, Kane placed down the tray, moving so he could brush his finger over Eli's bottom lip, almost ticklish but sensual at the same time. Another new strange sensation.

"I'm going to feed you," Kane purred.

Eli nodded, knowing he didn't have to reply with a "yes, Master" because Kane hadn't called him "boy". It was something he understood about their dynamic already.

"All right," was what he offered to a smile from Kane as the man kept his touch upon Eli's lips, delightful sensations the result.

Eli liked this.

After breakfast, one Eli enjoyed—really hearty and delicious actually, even though he wasn't so sure about being fed his food as if he was a toddler or something— Kane stood. Eli waited for him to speak, both curious and anxious now.

Kane whispered, "I want you to lie down on the daybed, boy."

He knew the response needed. "Yes, Master."

With a gentle breeze caressing the leaves of all the plants around him, thankfully not too cool, he found himself bathed in a pool of sunlight as he did as he was asked.

Eli squinted, the morning so bright and perfect already.

Kane sat on the daybed next to him after rearranging a few of the cushions, mostly to make Eli more comfortable. To also ensure he wasn't looking directly up, too. Eli appreciated that, indicating his thanks after Kane asked.

From there, almost like a dream, his surrounds making it more so, Eli's usual fawn-colored skin with pinkish undertones seemed brighter, seemed to almost glow because of the drenching sunlight. He felt contented, nervous, anxious, and strangely aroused all in one sticky mess within him right now, unsure what was going to happen next.

Eli began to fidget.

Thankfully, and without further delay, Kane leaned down so he could kiss Eli's flaccid dick gently with wetted lips, one, two, and three times. At that, Eli began to spiral immediately, unable to quantify at first such a sensation. His head spun and his skin tingled and tickled and became heated all at the same time, more so where he was kissed.

He also got a hard-on.

While Eli went through his processes, Kane kissed him there five, six, seven more times, all of them sending shivers of delight through Eli in sensual ripples. Unbelievable. Kane, to add even more to an already overwhelming experience, also ran his warm hand gently over Eli's already quivering stomach.

"You smell good, boy," the man said as his attention gained more purpose, as he began using his tongue too. "Nice and clean, but with the tangy hint of your matureness underlying that."

"Thank you...for your c-compliment, Master."

Eli looked down. His dick, all perked up as the intensity of the situation began to overwhelm him, was wet with Kane's affection, glistening in the light.

What a sight!

But when his Master gently pulled back Eli's foreskin to lick around his swollen knob to really give him strange but erotic feels, right to his balls, that's when he became completely overwhelmed. When he became pinned to the daybed, unable to do anything but become carried away, no lie. Eli, aside from squirming and quivering in delight, couldn't move. He most certainly couldn't feel his legs.

It was fantastic already.

And aside from the wonderful turmoil, what was with his heavy breathing all of a sudden?

"You please me," Kane added as he took Eli's dick completely into his mouth, easily.

If Eli was flying up to heaven because of Kane's lips and tongue upon his private place, the man's mouth engulfing it sent him into the stratosphere. To Eli, having never received a blowjob before, he could only describe the feeling like he was wearing a warm, wet, and sensual glove around his erection. One that sucked on it and moved in time with his ecstasy, too.

Eli found he couldn't hold back.

"Ahh! I'm…going to c-cum…Master!" he cried once the pit of his stomach began to swirl like a whirlpool within him.

What a rush!

And before he could add another moan, cry another "ahh!", inhale another hard breath, or beat another quickened heartbeat, Eli let go. Let go of everything with an almighty shudder.

Kane moaned as he took it all, swallowing every drop Eli delivered in four earth-shattering almighty squirts and three aftershocks that trembled through him.

When completely spent, sweating, Eli's vision slowly returned as he cooled but still exhausted from the sheer power of such a thing being done to him, Kane shuffled up the daybed to kiss Eli upon his cheek.

"I'm pleased that you're almost there."

Confusion found Eli. "I don't...understand."

Kane offered a gentle laugh. "You must eat well, because your flavor was almost to my liking—only a touch too salty."

"Oh...I see." Eli sat up. "That's a good thing, right?"

"It is."

Another kiss was given on Eli's cheek. He noticed, almost to his disappointment, that such affection was never delivered upon his lips, though. How could someone put another man's dick into their mouth, swallow his cum, too, yet not kiss him on his lips, either before or afterward?

That seemed strange to Eli.

He therefore felt a sudden urge to give his thanks to the man...no, to his Master who'd just pleasured him in a more appropriate way. Eli, feeling giddy again, nervous, too, closed his eyes before he closed the distance between them. A heartbeat later, another racing one all of a sudden, he ghosted his lips over Kane's. The man didn't shy away.

Eli took that as a good sign.

From there, he kissed Kane properly, lips pressed against lips and with his arms curling around the man's shoulders. To his delight, Kane held him back. They stayed connected for many uncountable delightful moments bathed in sunlight and warmed by not only nature but each other's company too.

When parted, almost breathless, certainly aroused again, Eli asked, "I'm sorry if what I did wasn't expected of me, Master. But I wanted to do that for you after what you did to me."

Kane bowed his head. "I didn't ask you to kiss me."

Eli suddenly feared he'd overstepped a line, still finding the whole Dom/sub dynamic a strange land yet to be fully discovered. "I'm sorry if I—"

"Don't be sorry."

Kane's eyes suddenly went watery, and he wiped them with the back of his hand. A pause then. Eli couldn't help but wonder if he was feeling the same emotions as he was after their first intimate moment together. More so, perhaps.

Before he could ask, Kane continued, "And you are most welcome to kiss me any time you desire it." A smile then, enigmatic and lovely. "I enjoyed it very much, thank you."

Eli, surprised now for a different reason, mostly because he was the one to have caused such a thing not the other way around, really had to ask, "You…you've…you've not been kissed like that before, have you?"

Kane got up, composing himself, clearing his throat, too. "I want you to drink a couple of glasses of pineapple juice I'll prepare for you momentarily, boy. It should take away some of the saltiness you have."

"Yes, Master."

Kane turned to leave, but not before adding, "After that, I'll need to run an errand which will mean I'll be gone for an hour. You are to stay here, boy. When I return, I'll feed you your lunch. Perhaps after that your taste will have improved and I can begin the next step of your training."

"Yes, Master."

Jiro felt even weaker than at any other time during his capture, the last dose of drugs injected into him against his will unfortunately seemed more potent than any of the others he'd been given. It took him ages to find a way out of his confusion. He really couldn't. And his fuzzy head pounded as if someone was hammering the back of his head.

While he was so worried about himself, naturally so, he felt the bed move beside him, the familiar creak of weight upon it. His heart stopped again for a moment, breath hitched, as he cursed that he hadn't heard his abuser enter the cell that time.

That he had no warning.

"Whathafuuuckdoyawantnoow?" Jiro slurred, realizing his muscles were still so relaxed from his intoxicated state that even his tongue rolled lazily around in his mouth when he tried to speak.

"Why, I'm here to relieve myself inside you, of course," his abuser said with a chuckle that grated on Jiro immediately. "Seeing as you're my fuck toy, why else would I be here?"

Jiro tried to look at the man. His neck muscles weren't working right either, and he was only able to catch a glimpse of that sinister silhouette he hated so much, right to his soul, within his peripheral vision.

"Fuuckoffff."

"My, my, is this is how you show your appreciation?

Even after I've personally cooked you a meal of eggs with furikake and a side of pickled vegetables, just so you can keep up your strength for me?"

"Whyyybootherrr?

"Don't sound so down. I can assure you I'll keep you alive for as long as you amuse me. And for now, you do so amuse me."

"WhaathappensswhenIdon'tammuuseyounomoore?"

"I'll put a gun to your head and pull the trigger." More light, amused laughter. "You won't even know it's been done, so painless and quick it is. I promise."

Jiro swallowed as best he could, fear once more gripping the parts of him he could feel. Which wasn't much. His head pounded worse than ever, and his whole body ached.

He was a helpless mess, and he hated that—but not as much as he hated the man who'd done this to him. Jiro had to hold back his tears as much as he could.

Overwhelmed, terribly so, his abuser fed Jiro the food he'd described, most of it falling off Jiro's chin to land on his chest seeing as he was unable to control his lips very well.

He couldn't taste what was given to him, either.

As far as Jiro was concerned, the food could have been either vile or a delight; he just didn't know. His drugged-up state muddled every sense, a deliberate thing, he knew.

When done, the man cleaned him up before Jiro felt another prick of a needle. Soon, and to his horror growing within him like a toxic plume, his abuser touched his dick before going lower with his attention.

"*Pleeeasenooo!*"

"Oh, how I love it when you beg me to not fuck you. Keep doing so, it's so arousing."

Just then Jiro, frightened but also in a deeper state of relaxation thanks to the drugs now affecting him even more, pissed himself as the inevitable happened.

Wednesday, 11:27 am

When Kane returned, Eli was ordered to wash and dry the breakfast dishes by hand. He was also required to clean the kitchen and mop the floor to a high standard too. Make it shine. Thankfully it wasn't a tiled floor but one of those fancy polished concrete deals with ground granite embedded within it.

Before he'd completed his task, wringing the mop out one last time before the final few swishes of it were needed, he swore he heard something strange coming from one of the floor's gratings.

Something that caused him to pause.

Cocking his head to hear better, because to him it sounded like a moan, of all things, he didn't hear it again. Eli then believed it was a figment of his imagination.

He shook his head.

That was a silly thing to think he'd heard moaning, truly. He knew that it was only Kane and him in the house. If they weren't alone, then surely Eli would have seen someone else by now. A gardener. A butler perhaps. But there'd been no one else other than the driver of the Mercedes. And he hadn't been seen since yesterday when Eli first arrived.

Eli shrugged, continuing on with his chores.

When done, he was to call for his Master to inspect his work. Kane did so, smiling and clearly pleased. Eli beamed a smile.

"You *have* done well, boy."

"Thank you, Master," Eli replied proudly, satisfied he'd pleased Kane.

He then, unexpectedly even to himself, gave Kane another kiss. A beautiful press of lips, giddy feelings, and going all weak at the knees as the result of it.

Kane blushed but didn't seem as flustered that time. "Thank you for that too," was all he returned, even if his voice wavered.

Eli held his smile.

And it was then he felt something strange within him. A feeling similar to butterflies but deeper. More profound. He couldn't quantify it, but to him it felt like…affection.

Affection for Kane so soon.

Wednesday, 1:47 pm

After lunch, a repast of noodles and stir-fried vegetables, followed by those lovely sweet rice dumplings Kane had carefully made for him the first time they'd met, Eli was instructed to once more lay down on the daybed.

Why not keep eating outside? The day was still beautiful. But it wasn't only the weather that made it so bright, Eli realized.

It was Kane.

This time, his Master wanted something different to happen. "I'd like you to now masturbate yourself for me, boy." It was then Eli noticed not all of the kibi dango had been eaten, a plate of four presented with an accompanying grin. "I desire to know what your ejaculate tastes like once it has seasoned these dumplings."

That was different.

Even though curious, at the same time Eli suddenly felt unsure. He'd never pleasured himself in front of anyone else before. He didn't even like looking at himself when he did it, ensuring the sheets and bedclothing covered him or he did it in the dark.

"Yes...Master," he answered even though his voice faltered, unable to disguise his discomfort.

Eli felt his cheeks warm.

Kane must have picked up on Eli's doubts. "There's no need to be embarrassed."

"I'm...not, honest." Eli swallowed. "I'm...I've just never liked touching myself because of...you know. How I see...myself."

"Oh, my heart." Kane's expression softened, and quickly he caressed Eli's cheek while moving so their lips were close, close enough to feel his breath. "Do you want to know how I see you?"

Eli shook his head. "I know you like me, otherwise I wouldn't be lying here naked in your garden..."

Kane snorted a light laugh, so like him. "My, my, you are just beautiful to me. And I honestly only see perfection when I gaze upon you. And I promise my words are the truth of my soul."

And from those words, clearly spoken from his heart, Kane crashed his lips onto Eli's. The moment was perfection. Perfection because Eli's breath was taken from him, stolen completely by the intention behind such intimacy all of a sudden.

He moaned deep from his throat.

Kane must have taken that as permission to deepen their contact, show the meaning and truth of his words on another level. With his arms enveloping Eli, bringing him into what he realized was his new safe place, he soon felt the man's tongue run over his lips.

The sensation was electric. Eli, tingling, going giddy already, opened his mouth for Kane. From there, it was all a euphoric haze. Eli shuddered, getting hard within seconds as their tongues connected them beyond what anything else could, he imagined. In truth, his heart raced, pounding out the rhythm of his desires for Kane.

And he couldn't help but realize the taste of Kane was the biggest surprise to him. Because, like him, Kane's mouth got wetter the more they kissed, the more they swapped saliva. Eli moaned even more, knowing his dick was leaking, loving that he was.

Loving even more that he'd been swept away by his Master's kiss.

When parted, Eli's lips still tingling, the rest of him wonderfully worse, Kane whispered, "Did you want me to masturbate you? I don't want you to ever feel uncomfortable; because as I begin to understand you, the more I realize this."

"I'd like that. Thank you…Kane." Eli wasn't sure if he should have addressed him by his name.

Kane didn't seem to mind, already grabbing Eli's

hardness. Clearly, his Master's focus was on making him happy now; a realization proven when Kane ran his fingers, gently so, over the tip of Eli's wet, with his own excitement, foreskin to really make the passion and feelings he felt grow with an even greater intensity.

Eli's pre-cum was then used to help lubricate what followed. He was completely at Kane's mercy. Again, loving that he was. He also loved being touched by another man in such a way, more than he would have believed he would. Mostly because the man doing it, his Master, seemed to care for him. Care for him a lot.

And that made all the difference.

"I'm...going to c-cum!" he soon cried.

Kane moved the plate of kibi dango so that Eli could squirt his sticky cum all over them, "season" them as he'd been told to refer to it. When Eli had done what he was asked to do, relieved and pleased, not really much of a chore at all, Kane began eating the dumplings.

It was mesmerizing to watch.

The man's smile turned profound when they'd been consumed, all four of them. "You are ready, I believe."

"I am?"

Kane nodded. "Tonight, and before dinner, we will begin your anal training for what I desire from you."

Eli, unable to help himself smiled. "I look forward to it."

From there, another beautiful, passionate, and wonderful kiss, deep and loving and with their tongues touching. Eli, overwhelmed again, panting almost, couldn't help but begin to get emotional.

Kane pulled away. "What's the matter, my heart?"

"I...I think...I *think* something's happened...I didn't expect."

A lovely smile now. A run of fingers over his heated skin. A gentle nod before his ear was kissed. "Tell me what you didn't expect," Kane breathed, sensually so.

"Please...call me your 'boy'...Master. To hear that now makes me feel...like I truly belong to you."

"You *do* belong to me, boy."

"*Yes*, Master, I do."

Kane held Eli tightly, really taking him to his safe place within his arms. Eli softly shed tears of joy there. "Then please tell me what it is you need to say to me, boy."

"I think I'm...I have feelings for you I didn't know I'd have for anyone else..."

"Are you saying you love me *already*?"

"As strange as it sounds, even to myself, I believe... that's what I'm s-saying, yes."

That time, Jiro heard the door open.

"You're a fucking monster!" he spat venomously before his abuser sat on the bed.

And even though he didn't seem as drug-affected, he was still in a bad way. Dribble ran down his chin, his head pounded, terribly so, and his body ached unbelievably. At the same time, the collar and chain fitted around his neck clinked and pulled on him whenever he moved, painfully rubbing his skin as he tried to move, tried to test its strength.

Jiro winced. But he admitted that was the first time he'd felt such pain from his restraints. Was his abuser reducing his dosage? Or was he becoming more resistant to it? He just didn't know.

"Oh, I'm much worse than that." His abuser's voice pierced through the gloom, only an outline of the man seen; his macabre and unfortunately familiar silhouette overtaking everything else.

And then there were those eyes.

Those terrible, evil eyes that glinted with want as they caught the waning light from the small, barred window above. Jiro tried to swallow his fear. He couldn't. And with growing dread, right to his stomach to make it squirm as much as he did, he then felt his abuser run his fingertips over his dick, tickle the lip of his foreskin with his poisonous touch, then cup his balls before squeezing them.

Jiro let out a yelp.

This was even more a living nightmare now it had gained more clarity for some reason.

With his voice still slurred, he managed, "What are you talking about? You...you can't be any worse than you already are, asshole."

His abuser snorted a mocking laugh. "Oh, you think drugging and then raping you every day is at the deepest depths of my depravity? No, no, there you are sadly mistaken. Sadly mistaken."

Terror struck Jiro even more, his heart thumping hard, mouth dry, and a cold sweat suddenly finding him. "What...do you m-mean?"

Without an immediate answer, Jiro heard movement,

then managed to catch a glimpse of the needle being prepared for him. His abuser humming to himself as he did so, as if it was nothing.

As if Jiro was nothing.

Which, he supposed he wasn't.

Not to this monster.

Jiro knew now without doubt the drug inside the syringe would soon relax him, send him into an almost unresponsive state, even if what happened to him after that would be horrific. Unimaginable. Because, once the drug's claws took hold on him again, he'd be easier to rape once more.

As he'd been raped many times already.

And as much as Jiro didn't want to give his abuser the satisfaction of seeing him cry, he couldn't help doing so. Not at all. Tears soon fell from his eyes to wet his cheeks, his sadness overwhelming him.

He then tried to do his best to disassociate himself. He failed. The drugs weren't working as much now. No longer helping him leave this nightmare while the unthinkable happened to him.

"What I mean," the man began, "is that I've made Eli fall in love with me. How very delicious, am I right?"

As soon as the words sunk in after a moment of them floating in his thoughts, Jiro felt as though he'd been punched. The wind knocked from him. "Eli? My...*brother* Eli, you mean?"

His abuser nodded. "The very same."

It was then that Jiro, with his eyes wide and lips trembling, tasting his own saltiness, too, began to cry even more. Great big dripping tears that made his shoulders heave he was so overwhelmed. Eli. His precious little brother was in the hands of this monster too.

Jiro was no longer in a nightmare. He was in hell and not alone there, either.

Poor Eli.

And if there was one thing...*one thing*...Jiro knew he had to do with every fibre of his being, that was to try his best to escape. He could no longer just give up. No longer accept his fate.

Eli needed him.

He *had* to get away. Knowing to his soul that he also had to save his little brother from the monster who used both of them for his sick and perverted pleasures.

"I'm going to kill you," Jiro spat. "Mark my fucking words."

"I very much doubt that...Jiro."

Jiro was stunned his abuser had called him by his name, the first time he'd done so. But before he could form any other coherent thought, the hope that'd sparked with him because he now had a purpose, even if he had no idea how he was going to accomplish it, was snuffed out instantly as soon as he felt the prick on his arm.

Jiro couldn't help it, he blurted, "No...*please*, no!"

As he expected, his plea made no difference.

Wednesday, 5:45 pm

The afternoon, languid and beautiful, was spent in the blissful wonderland of Kane's arms while they lay on the couch together watching old samurai movies—his Master's favorite genre. Eli loved being caressed and held as if he was the most important boy in the world. Which, right now, he was. He'd never felt so close to anyone before, not even Mason.

It was strange and delightful at the same time.

"I love you, Master," he whispered, surprising himself after Kane had kissed him deeply for the twenty-seventh time that day since their first true kiss.

Their first kiss, which still lingered on his lips, more potent than any that'd followed simply because it was the true beginning of how Eli felt about Kane.

Kane offered his intoxicatingly enigmatic smile. "And you are loved by me as well, boy."

Before these precious moments of delight, Eli completely smitten he knew, after lunch he'd completed his designated chores to his Master's satisfaction with joy in his heart.

They mostly involved kitchen clean-up, but he was also required to vacuum the bedroom's carpeting, wipe down the shower after Kane had taken his, and do some light dusting.

During that time, Kane had run another errand, returning one hour later; all his errands lasting that long, it seemed. Perhaps he was delivering food to someone, because Eli noticed how he seemed to cook a lot of it…well, there were always plenty of dishes, pot, pans, and utensils to wash and dry, anyway.

No matter.

Eli didn't want to question Kane. Not even when he heard that strange moaning sound again after he'd mopped the kitchen floor. One that stopped the minute he noticed it.

"For dinner, I've got something special planned," Kane said, bringing Eli back to the moment.

With his wettened lips close to his Master's, looking lovingly into his dark, dreamy eyes, Eli also semi-erect, leaking pre-cum, and overwhelmed, a common and welcome state lately, he replied, "What are you cooking for me?"

"I'm making you tonkatsu, boy."

Eli had heard of the deep-fried pork dish usually served with a special sauce and green vegetables, but had not had it. "I look forward to that, thank you, Master."

"Before you do shower and then prepare yourself for me more appropriately this time, I want you to fetch me a bottle of wine from the cellar—a lovely vintage German Riesling will do nicely as an accompaniment to the dish."

"Yes, Master."

"Good boy."

Eli got up, missing his Master's touch already. His warm, sensual lips most of all. Also, his warmth and his hold. Heck, Eli missed everything about him, really.

He didn't want to leave Kane.

But he knew he had to, never wanting to be disobedient, not deliberately, anyway. At that moment, something struck him as he looked at the solid wooden door beyond the lounge room.

It was closed.

He gulped. "Do I have your permission to open the doors I need to so I can do as you've asked me, Master?"

"You do." Kane sat up, reaching to touch Eli reassuringly on his bare buttocks. "The cellar is beyond the kitchen and down a staired hall beyond the larder. It's on the left. The door to the right is locked. Do not attempt to open it, you don't have my permission to go in there."

"I'll only go to the cellar as you've instructed, Master."

Kane nodded. "You really do please me, boy."

"Thank you, Master."

Eli left the loungeroom.

Where he was told to go, that's where he unfortunately discovered his first true obstacle since arriving at Kane's home. One he didn't expect, to be honest.

It was one of his worst fears, actually.

Eli, as he stared at what lay beyond the door from the kitchen, began to sweat despite his nakedness and the cooler air in the lower parts of the house.

He simply stood there for ages staring, unable to move.

When he did, forcing himself to, he muttered, "I can't…go into that hallway."

Eli then stepped back, his head spinning as he saw the mosaic-tiled flooring beyond—so many joins to avoid, he knew he wouldn't be able to cope with them all.

He backed away.

At that moment, his back found a barrier to his retreat. Thankfully it was Kane. The man, his beautiful Master, quickly holding him tightly from behind as Eli pressed his body against his warmth, his rapid heartbeats returning to a steadier pace.

Kane asked, "Are you all right?" as he turned Eli around so they were facing.

"The floor, it's too…triggering for me."

Kane looked at him, then to the hallway. "How so?"

"The tiles…the joins, I mean. I can't deal…with them. They…it's f-from when I was b-beaten and left on a tiled floor. I can't…"

"Hush, my heart." Kane kissed his forehead tenderly, holding him tighter. "I'm here for you now."

"I'm…such a m-mess," Eli began to feel his tears well, sting his eyes. Thank God, Kane was there to hold him, bring him into his safe place, kiss him more deeply and lovingly as well.

And kiss they did.

Eli found he didn't cry, after all. Kane had done that—stopped his tears from flowing. Eli's love and trust for him as well had done it, too.

"I wondered why you sometimes flinched when I made a sudden move. Now I know," Kane said gently when he broke their kiss. "I'll try to never do that again, boy."

"Thank you, Master."

"Now, did you want me to put a hall runner down for you?" Kane asked, again another kiss given, not as deep but just as appreciated. "That way you won't have to walk on the tiles."

"You'd do that for me?"

"I'd do anything for you."

Eli almost swooned, and found himself once more

wrapped in his Master's warm, beautiful embrace. His true safe place.

Wednesday, 7:12 pm
After dinner, Eli was told to once more lie down.

The evening had become cool, a light rain pattering against the window panes, so Kane suggested the next step of Eli's training be done in the warmth of the house. In the comfortable lounge room with massive suede couches and plenty of scatter cushions.

When Eli was in position, no longer anxious and actually able to relax for the first time in memory, Kane the reason, asked, "Did you clean yourself as I asked you to, boy?"

"Yes, I did, Master."

Kane kissed Eli's lips; Eli already falling into bliss by such a simple but profound gesture. A gesture he craved and loved when given. "I'm pleased, as I knew I would be."

"Can I ask what you're going to do to me this time?" Eli hoped his Master would fuck him...or at least offer himself so Eli could suck his dick. He'd not seen his Master naked yet.

No matter what happed he was prepared, mentally most of all.

"You can." Kane caressed Eli's cheek. "I'm going to enhance your taste."

Okay, Eli, as he'd been so much already, became confused and *wasn't* prepared for that sort of response. "I...I don't understand. How?"

"Do you trust me?"

"With everything I am," Eli replied without hesitation, getting emotional too. He really did trust Kane.

Another kiss, one deeper and wanted because it reassured Eli before Kane ordered, "Open your legs for me, boy—you'll soon feel the overwhelming carnal delights of a prostate massage."

Eli was intrigued. "Oh…yes, Master."

Kane produced what Eli assumed was lube. From there, and rather seductively he found, his Master slicked his long fingers with the clear, thick drizzling fluid from the bottle. The squelching noise of it while Kane covered his fingers with it suddenly turned up the warmth within the lounge room, no lie. Eli licked his lips in anticipation.

"I'll insert one finger first; if it hurts you let me know, boy."

"I will." Eli nodded. "And I'm ready for this, Master."

Eli closed his eyes to immerse himself in the experience. To his joy, he soon felt Kane's touch caress his anus, move his fingers in little circles to send strange sensations all through him to settle at the base of his spine.

New feelings, simply because someone other than himself was doing it to him. A delight. And once Eli became accustomed to being touched there, the vulnerability he imagined he would have felt not present, he moaned, giving his Master the sign that he was ready for more.

So much more.

Without delay, Kane pushed the tip of one of his fingers inside Eli, piercing him, owning him even more, he believed. His moan became a forced intake of air as the result of his Master's actions strengthened the sensations to an even deeper level.

But that was nothing compared to what happened next.

Once Kane began to feel inside Eli, finding the exquisite place easily because of Eli's arousal—to have it palpated, rubbed, teased, circled, and pressed against—it sent shockwaves of delight all through him.

"Ahh!" Eli cried with shuddering pleasure, arching his back. "Oh, God! Mhm! Ahh!"

Kane kept up his purpose, Eli loving that he did. Needing him too, because as his mind became a hazy miasma of pleasure that'd all come from his Master's concentrated touch.

And what a touch that was.

Eli, mouth agape, saliva dripping, moaning, groaning, tingling everywhere except where he went numb, quivered and writhed around Kane's finger.

"You're so tight, boy."

"L-loosen…me up, M-Master!" Eli trembled as Kane rubbed with more intent. "Pleeease!"

Kane did so. Eli felt the stretch as he was opened by another finger entering him, the delightful ferocity of it adding to his already overwhelmed state.

"More?"

Eli's eyes were watering, and along with the pleasure there was now an unsettling pain radiating from where he'd been penetrated. A pain unlike any other. "E-enough…for n-now…"

Kane then settled into a rhythm with his touch inside

Eli, the pain dissipating as he began to relax once more. But with the fall of his hurt, the inevitable rise of everything else followed.

"I can see your balls tighten, boy!"

Eli was close, no denying that because it was written all over his sweating, heaving body. "I'm…I'm g-going to cum s-soon!"

"Hold off for a long as you can."

Eli tried to. He did. But with the sensations so powerful within him, he fought hard to do as he was told. "I'll…t-try!"

As Kane massaged Eli's prostate, Eli at his complete mercy through such an erotic and wonderful touch, he thought about how he was an extension of his Master.

The Master and his boy as one.

Because yes, that was what Eli was. He belonged to his Master, wonderfully so. He was needed. Desired. Pleasured and pleased in equal measure too. He was also owned. As such, he was truly in love, the safest and most wanted he'd been in his life. All because of Kane.

With an almighty shudder, cries of ecstasy, too, spittle flying, back arching as far as it would go, arms and legs numb, Eli came.

And came…

And came…

By the time he realized Kane's warm, sucking mouth was around his dick taking it all, Eli was done. Exhausted and loving that he was.

When Kane came off Eli, he licked his lips. "Your taste is as perfect as you are."

Eli, flushed from the internal massage, almost incoherent because of the result of it, managed, "Th-thank…you."

Kane kissed Eli.

The taste of himself another overwhelming thing. So tangy and salty but also sweet. The taste of him Kane wanted, no doubt. Eli was glad he could provide.

Really glad.

Once more, and after six more deep kisses accompanied with loving embraces, wandering hands, and more arousal on Eli's part, Kane parted. Close, lip to lip close, he whispered, "I want you to wait for me in the bedroom, boy."

"Yes, Master."

"I will join you when I've ran my last errand for the day."

"I understand," Eli replied without question, even though he wondered why so many errands had to be done today, three of them now.

"Good boy."

Wednesday, 10:36 pm

Kane returned after a longer than usual absence, forty-seven minutes more than the hour he was always gone for. And even though Eli wasn't worried, he *had* become concerned.

So concerned he couldn't sleep.

All of those concerns were quickly washed away, however, when his Master crawled into their bed next to him and held Eli tightly.

No word.

No sound.

Nothing other than a warm engulfing safety Eli certainly felt when within Kane's embrace. If he wasn't mistaken, he believed Kane had missed him. Missed him a lot. Because he seemed to be sucking back his emotions too, Eli feeling the little shudders of them through their contact.

Eli didn't ask about such things though.

From nowhere Kane whispered, "I love you, too," while his lips caressed the shell of Eli's ear, delightfully so. "And I've told you that because when you said that you loved me earlier, I didn't return it properly. Now I have. I love you, Eli Shigeru, my boy, my heart. I love you unlike anyone I've loved before in my life."

Eli now felt his emotions stir, needing a moment to compose himself. Kane held him tighter, obviously sensing his state of being.

Why wouldn't he?

Eli was his boy and Kane had certainly learned so much about him already. More than what even Eli knew about himself, to be honest.

From there, Eli slept peacefully in his Master's arms. And for the first time in memory, he didn't dream of that day that left him hospitalized. He dreamt of the joy in his heart he had for Kane.

His undying love.

The Fourth Day

1.4: By signing the Dom/sub contract, boy gives explicit consent to be used how Master sees fit, sexually and/or otherwise. Consent can only be withdrawn if boy feels as though he may be hurt or injured. Master will respect his boy's concerns.

Jiro hazily remembered he'd cried for a long time. He also remembered he wasn't visited again that day since his abuser had brought him in his lunch, drugged him, then used him for his pleasure before hosing him and the plastic sheet-covered mattress down. The water was always freezing cold.

He shivered at that.

But Jiro didn't know whether such an absence was a good thing or a bad one. Although at that, his muddled thoughts suddenly turned terribly to Eli's welfare.

"I'll do whatever I can to save you, Eli," he said to no one before he had no choice but to relieve himself and then sit within his own filth until the monster came calling again.

Thursday, 7:06 am
Eli woke to an empty bed.

When Kane entered the bedroom one minute later,

fully dressed and carrying a breakfast tray, he said cheerily, "Good morning, boy."

"Good morning, Master," Eli returned, matching the intent.

He then stretched.

"You may attend to your personal duties before joining me in our private garden. I want you to do for me what I truly desire today. You are most certainly ready for it."

Eli nodded. "Thank you…" But he paused for a moment, considering whether or not he should voice the question swirling within his thoughts.

Kane, picking up on Eli's hesitation, asked, "What bothers you, boy?"

"I was…if I may ask, where you were, Master?"

Kane immediately replied, "I was conducting business with a few of my associates." He put the breakfast tray down onto the dresser with care, as he always did everything. He turned to Eli. "I've invited them here for dinner tonight to complete the deal I've been negotiating over for the past few months. I have finally secured a new restaurant—my old one got burnt down, you see."

Eli nodded, but gulped. "I see." But he wasn't so sure all of a sudden, mostly because he didn't know what was expected of him in company. How he was to present himself? What he was to do?

Did he have to do anything?

Kane's expression softened. "You're worried about what they'll think of you, aren't you?" He offered his open arms, to which Eli got up off the bed to fall into without thought. "I can see the concern all over your face."

"I...am."

"They will love you like I do."

Eli felt his Master's warmth permeate him to his soul. "What...what do you want me to do for you tonight, Master?"

Kane pulled Eli away to look him in his eyes. "I want you to serve them their food and drinks and continue being the perfect boy that I know you are, okay?"

Eli, captivated, lost within Kane's attention, and feeling better for it, replied, "I'd love to do that for you." He paused...suddenly feeling the pressure of his further thoughts within him wanting to emerge. "But...."

"But what, my heart?"

"Did you...you know...want me to remain naked...or can I wear clothing?"

"My, my, that's entirely up to you." Kane kissed Eli's lips. "But whatever you decide, just know that because you are mine, they will not touch you in any way no matter what. They will only respect you. I promise."

Eli certainly liked the sound of that. He was also more confident in himself because Kane was with him. "I think I'll stay...I'd like to remain naked. For you and only for you, though."

"You *are* amazing, you know that, boy?"

"Thank you, Master."

Another kiss, deeper and longer.

Eli was glad he'd pleased his Master. And yes, even though he was nervous about others seeing him with nothing on, that really didn't matter in the end. Kane needed him to be a perfect boy, so that's what he'd be.

And everyone could see that too.

After all, for his Master to get his new restaurant and Eli playing a part of it, trusted to do so, too, that was a wonderful feeling.

Simply wonderful.

Kane, his lips wet with Eli's love, added, "I would also like it if you were to season the kibi dango for the guests tonight after dinner. The restaurant's concept is to provide such a service for the higher paying guests."

"I don't want—"

"No one will touch you." Kane ran his gentle touch down Eli's back to reassure him, which it did. It so did. "I'll be the one who'll masturbate you for your precious and tasty ejaculate. That's my promise, and my promise is my promise. That much should never be in doubt, my heart."

"I don't doubt you. Not at all." Eli breathed. "But will they watch you doing that to me?"

"Did you want them to?"

"I'm not sure," Eli replied honestly, nerves bubbling though.

"Then I won't pressure you. You can decide tonight after you've realized how much they will adore you and how grateful they'll be no matter what."

"Thank you, Master."

Thursday, 10:28 am
After Eli had answered nature's call and showered, he went to Kane as he'd been asked to do. The French doors

to their private garden were wide open, letting the air into the house, so he didn't have to ask permission to open them.

One less worry.

Because ever since Kane had told him there would be guests tonight, Eli's mind had turned over and over with the possibilities of what could happen. Nothing negative, which was nice—and a change from his usual state of mind—but more about how he really wanted to impress. Impress his Master most of all.

Please him too.

As he entered the private garden, its beautiful scents finding Eli, Kane greeted him with a warm smile, as warm as he was sitting in the sunlight bathed in nature's glory.

"Are you ready for me to feed you your breakfast, boy?"

Eli sat on the cushioned chair just for him. "I am, Master."

"This morning, I have prepared for you a dish of komochi shishamo, the fish bearing plenty of roe too. I made sure of it."

Eli looked down at the two pristine white plates in front of his Master. Upon them, carefully placed on each, were seven small grilled fish accompanied by a neat mound of grated daikon. Next to that was a platter piled high with twenty-four kibi dango on a bed of banana leaves. Eli wondered why there were so many dumplings, but didn't question it.

"I've not eaten whole fish like this before," he said.

"They are delicious, my heart."

"Then I know I'll enjoy it, but mostly because you cooked them for me."

And Eli did enjoy his breakfast; the taste of the fish flavorsome in a braised and slightly salty kind of way. He was also getting used to the idea of being fed. More so since the activity involved Kane touching his lips and kissing him tenderly between bites.

It all became very sensual.

He really was in a beautiful world woven by everything Kane did. Every detail. Every care. Eli thought about how one month with Kane wouldn't be enough, really. He realized he wanted to be his Master's boy for as long as he could.

Longer than that...

When breakfast was eaten, Kane dabbing Eli's mouth with a napkin, gestured toward the daybed. He knew what to do, and lay upon it without being asked.

Kane picked up the platter of dumplings. "I want you to kneel for me instead of lying down this time, boy."

"Yes, Master." Eli, curious as to why, did as he was asked though.

"That's better." His master then produced a condom from his jacket's pocket along with a syringe. "Did you want me to masturbate you, or did you want to do it yourself this time? Remember, there's nothing to worry about, I'll always have your best interest at heart, boy."

Eli loved hearing those words, but at the same time was also now extremely curious. He began, "I'd like it if you masturbated me, please." But he couldn't hold back.

"But…um, what's the condom and syringe for, if I may ask, Master?"

"You may always ask questions—never think that you can't." Kane's softened expression revealed the truth of his words. "And to answer you, I want to capture your ejaculate within the condom." He began opening the packet. "That way, I can then use the syringe to draw it up easier."

"And then what?"

Kane smiled deliciously. "I'll inject your own cum into your ass."

"Okaaay." Eli swallowed. "Then w-what happens?"

"To get the delicacy I truly desire from you, you'll then begin inserting the kibi dango into yourself so that they'll become marinated by your juices inside you."

Eli felt a bit strange all of a sudden. "I…don't understand."

"The dumplings seasoned by your ejaculate are a treat worth any price, but to eat them after they've been inside you, that would be a culinary wonder."

"No, I mean…why can't you put *your* cum into me instead of using my own to flavor the dumplings?"

Kane's eyebrows rose slightly. "My, my, did you want me to fuck you, boy?"

"Yes, I really *do* want you to fuck me, Master. Why would I not want that?"

"My ejaculate would ruin them; it doesn't have the right taste."

"Oh," Eli offered, dejected. "I see."

Kane placed his hand under Eli's chin, forcing him to

look his Master in the eyes. Eli shivered, already feeling lost within them as he stared lovingly at his Master. "You please me so much, just know that."

"Then...why don't you want to fuck me?" Eli realized he was hard, achingly so because he was so full of yearning for Kane. "Look at me...I'm yours and I want you so, so much. Please, *please* take me, Master. I need your dick inside me. Please. I can't wait any longer. *Please*."

"How can I resist you when you speak like that, my heart?"

"I don't *want* you to resist me," Eli implored. "I want you to own me with all you have because I'm yours. I want you to fuck my ass while you fuck my mouth with your tongue at the same time." At that, Eli opened his mouth to emphasize his full and complete submission, body trembling and his tongue dripping with saliva because of his arousal.

He needed Kane to have him in all ways.

He'd waited too long.

"Then I *will* have you, boy." Kane placed two fingers into Eli's mouth, spreading his cheeks apart from the inside to really open it. "I will give every hole you have all the pleasure you desire and deserve, and I'm sorry if you thought I didn't desire you in all ways."

Eli moaned deep from his throat as Kane explored his mouth with his touch, slicking his fingers with Eli's growing arousal, turning him on even more at the same time. He didn't have to look. He knew he was leaking from his dick too as his heart raced and he could feel his breaths become uneven.

He was truly ready.

Within a delicious moment, full of loving stares into each other's eyes, Kane gently lay Eli upon the daybed proper. His Master made sure he was comfortable with the cushions placed just so, all the while caressing and kissing him. "You are the most beautiful boy I've ever seen."

Eli trembled under his Master's attention. "And you are so handsome, I can't think of anyone else I'd want to give myself to."

"Am I your first?"

Without hesitation, Eli replied, "You are."

"This news pleases me." Kane beamed a smile while still caressing Eli, as always. "And I now know the moment is right, because after I've fucked you, your hole will be nice and loose for the kibi dango to be inserted without breaking up their shape. I will enjoy them even more."

"My hole, my mouth, and my body are yours to do with as you please, now and for as long as you desire me."

"I'll always desire you, for you are the only boy I've ever truly loved."

Eli trembled with an even greater longing, feeling his emotions well at the same time, eyes watering. "And you are...m-my only love too."

"Then let's not waste any more time, boy."

"No, Master, let's n-not."

But first, Kane rolled the condom onto Eli's rock-hard dick, ensuring his foreskin was pulled back fully to keep the sensations as vivid as possible for what was to follow, something Eli appreciated.

After he'd been fucked, he knew he'd be ready for what his Master wanted of him even more. But for now, he'd get what *he* wanted. Truly wanted. Finally.

And that made all the difference.

With Eli writhing on the daybed consumed by his yearning anticipation, prickling his skin as well as heating it, his Master got up off it so he could remove his exquisitely made silken trousers. When they were untied and dropped, the sight of Kane's bulge underneath his underwear, stretching the material, was breathtaking. Eli could clearly make out the outline of his erection, a lovely little wet patch where the end of his knob was shown.

Kane slipped off his robe.

To make him even more desirable, to witness his fine form, his abdominal muscles prominent, pecs defined magnificently, turned Eli on even more. All he could imagine was being underneath such masculine beauty. Possessed by such beauty too. Wonderfully so.

"I *need* you, Master," Eli said shuddering, almost panting, knowing he soon *would* be owned in all ways, thank God.

Kane tugged down his underwear. His dick now revealed, sprang up. Eli sucked in a sharp breath, amazed. It was massive. A magnificent throbbing appendage, cut, oozing precum, and with bulging veins that seemed to ripple all over the length of its eight-inch plus shaft. Eli wanted it. No. He *needed* all of it inside him, right now.

He was about to say such a thing, when Kane commanded, "I want you to lick my cock to get it dripping wet for you, boy."

"Yes, Master!"

"Then I'm going to have you until you see the stars and my love and nothing else."

"That's all I want to see!" Eli, no longer able to hold back, sat up, grabbing his Master's dick eagerly, loving the girth, feel, and heat of it in his grip.

Now was the time to really be his Master's good boy.

Kane moaned. "Mhm...yes!" he hissed through his teeth as he threw back his head while he was touched so sexually, his Master obviously needing it as much as Eli did.

Which was awesome.

Eli squeezed Kane's dick harder, really making Kane's glistening apple-sized knob deepen to an arousing shade of crimson. "I love it!" he mouthed as he began tonguing his Master's length, his saliva already dribbling onto his chin.

Kane moaned more gutturally as Eli enjoyed what was offered to him, loving the taste, salty and tingling on his tongue to the back of his throat, as much as the knowledge that he now pleased his Master on a far more intimate level than he'd ever done.

When Kane's dick was dripping wet, as required and desired, he pulled away from Eli's attention. "Lie down, boy," he growled with yearning clear in his voice.

"Yes, Master!"

Eli soon found himself in a dream-like state, sunlight dappling all around as Kane came over him, became his world. Even more wonderfully, the journey to Eli's lips and the deep tongue kisses that would result, was a trail of his Master's attention all over his body. A path that began at his trembling balls but soon ended at his erect nipples, worshipped in turn, before finishing at his, soaked with his efforts, chin. He was covered in wet lines, a sensual roadmap of Kane's desire for him that Eli loved the sight of over his heated skin.

Within a heartbeat, Kane crashed his lips against Eli's.

More moans, that time from the both of them in unison as they held each other, hands desperately raking over skin, shudders and sharp intakes of breaths through flared nostrils, too. At the same time, he opened his mouth for his Master, his reward soon given for his submission.

His Master's tongue consumed him.

For the longest time they kissed wet, passionate, and sucking kisses that took Eli's breath away. Sent him into a spin already. During which time, Kane had moved so he was between Eli's legs proper.

Kane took a moment.

A moment before the storm! For Eli quickly felt an intense pressure between his legs right below his balls, groaning even more, before Kane thrust with a grunt and Eli's ass was pierced. Shit! A louder moan and a break of contact where Eli could then yelp. And yelp he did as Kane's massive knob was pushed into him with a painful pop.

"Oh, God!" Eli cried.

Kane backed off. "Are you all right, my heart?"

Eli, eyes watery again, shuddering with both pain and pleasure, nodded. "Keep g-going…please!"

From there, and as Eli relaxed, understanding what to expect, Kane gained his rhythm. They were one. Completely each other's. Utterly consumed. Wonderfully loved.

And Eli couldn't be happier.

And despite the initial awkwardness, he'd quickly learned to move in time with his Master, opening his legs and arching his back in a certain way so he could control the depth Kane's dick went inside him with more accuracy. Not that he wanted to. He wanted Kane in him *always*, deeply so, even though he knew that wouldn't be possible. He couldn't be fucked all the time.

Eli could dream though, right?

An age passed as their contact, their tongues, their sweat, their breaths, and their connection most of all solidified even more. Or seemed to. That's how Eli felt, anyway.

Although it was true, Eli did see stars as he felt the burn within him, deep and wonderful, while Kane pounded and pounded; the slapping sounds of him doing so even more arousing. Eli was his. His to use. Always.

At that thought, wonderful blinking stars surrounded Kane as Eli began to lose feeling in his legs. It was so beautiful to think about how he knew he wouldn't be able to stand after this.

Not for a while, anyway.

And it was also true that Eli also only saw Kane, a man who was not only his Master but his lover in the truest sense of the word now as well.

He loved that thought most of all.

Because Eli, filled, satisfied, climbing the heights to his own climax, consumed, dizzy, and wonderfully overloaded, every sense, couldn't hold back any longer.

He came.

"Ah! Ah! Ahhhh!" He shuddered and shuddered as he gave all he could into the condom, clenching his ass around his Master's dick as he orgasmed, his fists clenched, toes curled, and with dripping sweat off his brow because he'd been so close to his Master's carnal heat.

Delightfully close.

Kane soon added his chorus to Eli's, not far behind with his release. Eli knew this because his fervor had also gained purpose, his hold and kisses even more intense. Eli was pleased because it was his body that'd brought Kane to this.

But Kane didn't ejaculate inside Eli.

At the right moment, he pulled out to squirt his thick, sticky cum all over Eli's balls, dick, and stomach, so hot, while shuddering, eyes squeezed tight, and complete with that lovely "O" face to really make it amazing.

Yes, he'd done that to his Master.

But as much as he wanted Kane's cum inside him, Eli understood why—it *would* spoil the taste of the dumplings. But even so, it *would* have been something to have. Something that would make him even more Kane's.

Owned in every possible way as well.

When Kane sat up, wiping his brow, smiling, Eli then realized he still felt the sensation of his Master's dick inside him. A weird feeling. Mostly because in contrast, he also felt hollow and sore. Like the part of him that was suddenly missing had been torn out of him. A silly thing to think, but that's how he felt.

He did know one thing for certain though. Eli wanted to be fucked again already.

"You were wonderful," Kane whispered, reaching over to grab what he now obviously desired. "But now I want you to do as I've asked of you, boy."

"Yes, Master," Eli replied dreamily, sitting up as best he could, considering his body still raged with his ecstasy.

His hands trembled.

Everything trembled, really.

"Bless you." At that, the platter piled high with kibi dango was offered to Eli with a ceremonious bow. "I want you to insert these into yourself, please. All of them." No other expression was given other than the obvious lust he held in his eyes like a twinkle of life and the love he had for Eli.

So much love, it radiated off him to warm Eli greater than the sunlight.

A moment of pause, a lick of lips, a swallow. "So… you want me to put…*all of them*…into my ass, Master? All twenty-four?"

"Yes, I do, boy. *All of them*…if you can." Kane smiled. "Then, when your guts are full of the bounty I've gifted you, the kibi dango warmed enough by your body and marinated by your jizz I'll now put into you as well, that's when I want you to expel them for me so we can feast upon them together. Our shared meal you've helped prepare with your body, making it special and a part of us both, will be our reward for what we've done here today."

"We eat them together?"

"Yes."

Eli wasn't sure. "But I—"

"Please, do this for me and I will reward you again tonight once our dinner guests have departed."

Eli knew what that meant, and his uncertainty left him. "Yes, Master."

While Kane injected Eli's cum into his ass after he carefully removed the condom, Eli still hard, he picked up one of the dumplings placed just so on a bed of banana leaves that were plated together intricately, beautifully presented, from off the gilded and ornately patterned plate. The kibi dango were both soft and firm at the same time in his hand, like gelatine-made eggs really.

He moved to spread his legs, reveal his gaping freshly fucked hole to Kane to begin doing as he was told. Eli felt himself stir. The thought that what he was about to do would please his Master even more the reason.

The only reason that was more than enough for him.

Eli carefully pushed the first dumpling into himself, the delicacy going in easier than he would have believed. Already he could feel it inside him, pressing against his sensitive prostate after being so stimulated by Kane's rubbing, thrusting dick, making him leak with excitement already. He quivered delightfully, feeling heat rush through him.

His cheeks burned as a result.

"Are you embarrassed I'm watching you do this?" Kane purred, running his hands over Eli's legs in encouragement, brushing the hair on them with his fingertips.

"No, Master, I'm not." Another quiver when he inserted the next kibi dango into himself. "I'm excited because of what I'm doing for you."

"Good boy."

By the time Eli got to the eighteenth dumpling, the pressure inside him almost became too great, he stopped. His body wanted to expel them, that familiar feeling of wanting to shit taking over his senses. He really did feel full now.

"You're almost there," Kane observed, eyes glistening.

"I feel like I'm a turkey being stuffed for Christmas," Eli said, not in complaint but as an observation; the pressure inside him *was* building to the point of bursting.

He honestly didn't know how much longer he could keep his butt clenched, especially when he had to relax himself to get another dumpling up in there.

But he'd try.

Kane kissed Eli's stomach just above his recently trimmed pubic hairline. "I want you to put in as many as you can."

"I'll do my best."

"That's all I ask." Kane kept kissing Eli there. "I can feel how much your belly has distended because of the kibi dango inside you. And that's so very pleasing to me, boy."

"I am glad you're pleased, Master."

"That I am."

Eli inserted another dumpling, concentrating hard not to eliminate them but keep them all in there. He had to admit, his dick didn't soften, his arousal unabated despite what he did.

When he got to the twentieth one, he had to say, "I… can't insert any more into me, Master."

Kane kissed Eli. "You've done well." He took the platter away from Eli, placing it onto the table. "Now hold them in for a moment, let them marinade nicely inside you, boy."

"Yes, Master."

While he waited, Kane kept on kissing, holding, and caressing Eli. It was a strange, almost surreal movement knowing there were dumplings inside him while he was given so much affection. Many times, he had to clench to keep them inside himself, wincing, not from pain, but from the overwhelming urges coursing through his body.

He wouldn't be able to hold them in much longer.

Kane, thankfully, then parted his kiss to bring one of the plates over to Eli that had had the grilled fish on it. "The kibi dango will be ready now, I believe."

Eli nodded. "I think so too."

His Master once more came between Eli's legs. "You may begin expelling the dumplings, my heart."

Relieved, Eli replied, "That I sure will." And as he did so, the sensation exactly like taking a shit, Kane's face brightened even more, clearly happy.

When done, Eli a little tired from all the activity lately, he admitted, sat back up. Kane revealed the plate of twenty uniquely seasoned kibi dango.

They didn't look any different to Eli, which he

considered a good thing. Because yes, he was sure glad he'd cleaned himself properly in the shower earlier.

Really glad.

His Master popped the first dumpling into his mouth, smiling after he'd swallowed it. Eli, still unsure, didn't get time to consider such things though. Kane offered him the next one he'd picked up.

"Enjoy your bounty, boy."

Eli took it. "Yes, Master."

After which he looked at it, gulped, finally shrugged, then bit down on the warm, chewy dumpling that'd been inside his ass. If he told Mason about this, he wouldn't be believed. No way.

"Well? Kane asked, expectation in his expression as he leaned forward, selecting another dumpling for consumption at the same time. "What does it taste like?"

Eli admitted, aside from the saltier taste because of his own cum, there wasn't much else he could say other than the kibi dango tasted like… kibi dango. "I can taste myself, for sure."

"Yes, the taste of you is most delicious." Kane nodded. "And are you getting the after taste, the pungency once the sweetness and saltiness has been cleansed from the palate?"

Eli wasn't. "Not really," he hated to admit when he was offered another dumpling.

Kane smiled. "No matter—your palate is young and there is plenty of time to refine it. Nevertheless, I'm most pleased with them as I am most pleased with you."

His Master offered a bow.

Eli felt himself blush. "I'm just pleased you're pleased."

Jiro was woken by the door opening and his abuser's presence coming close to him. Creepily close. He heard the hose being turned on; the squeak of the faucet's handle unmistakable.

A moment after that, he was blasted with cold water.

"Leave me *the fuck* alone!" he yelled, his head thumping and his body shaking uncontrollably, both from the freezing water and the drugs swirling within him.

"You can lie here in your own filth if you prefer." The man then began washing Jiro, a strong disinfectant smell overtaking everything else. "Makes no difference to me."

"Fuck off!"

Jiro was dried with a towel, noting how his abuser's attention was concentrated on his ass and dick. He shivered, but now for a different reason. That was the routine now, it seemed—he'd get hosed down, washed, dried, fed, then raped. Jiro wanted this to end, do the unthinkable. Only he knew he couldn't do that to himself, even if there was a means to do so.

There was Eli to consider.

When done, Jiro, still shaking, turned to look at the monster. "I don't think you really care what happens to me."

"Oh, you're so wrong."

"How so?"

"Let me show you."

Jiro tried to back away, knowing all too well what would follow. The chain pulled on him, tugging hard, the collar hurting where it rubbed even more to make him wince. He couldn't get away. Knew he couldn't.

It was worth trying, though.

But what happened next wasn't what he expected. With the monster still standing over him, the man tugged down his pants to quickly reveal his hard-on.

Jiro's stomach turned terribly.

Not only was his abuser's dick an ugly monstrosity—just like him—all veiny and with a dried-up looking knob that leaked a dew drop of his clear excitement, but it was cut too. The scar was a jagged line, also ugly. Whatever doctor circumcised the bastard, they were a butcher.

Jiro couldn't help but see the amusing side of that. He would have, too, if he wasn't chained and in a living hell. He would have laughed his ass off.

His abuser, jolting Jiro out of his thoughts, said, "I want you to taste your brother's ass on my cock. That'll then give you the pleasure of knowing firsthand how I fuck him and how much he loves that I do." Another chuckle. "See? That's how much I care about you, Jiro. I want to keep all this in the family for you."

Jiro sucked in a sharp breath, his insides in turmoil now. "You really *are* a fucking monster."

The man laughed more menacingly, coming closer, his dick almost touching Jiro's lips. "You'll suck my cock while Eli's scent is still fresh on it, or I'll pump you so full of drugs I'll then do what I want with you while you're unconscious. Your choice."

Jiro's insides turned with his sudden fear, knowing the truth of the man's words. Knowing that if he was drugged like that, he may not live through the experience.

He was already affected enough by them, so weak and everything aching unbelievably whenever he moved.

But Jiro had to throw one more defiant barb before he knew he'd have no choice but to submit to the perverted man's wishes. "What? You're not going to rape me anymore?"

"No, I won't. Eli's ass is the only one I want now that I've had it."

Jiro swallowed hard. Poor Eli. But no matter what happened. What he had to suffer, he had to stay alive long enough to save Eli. How exactly he'd accomplish that, he didn't know. But seeing as things had changed, the routine broken, Jiro had a feeling his opportunity may come sooner than he thought.

"You like my brother, don't you?" he asked.

A dreamy look overcame the man. "I do." A blink as he must have returned to himself. "But stop trying to delay, Jiro. Get my cock into your mouth and suck my balls dry. Or else!"

The temptation to bite his abuser's dick off was great.

Thursday, 5:45 pm

Kane fussed over Eli for at least an hour before the first guest arrived. During that time, he'd made sure Eli's hair was brushed and gelled, his pubes and pits trimmed to an even shorter length, and his body was lightly oiled with a fragrant frangipani lotion that wasn't greasy but left his skin all shiny.

"My, my, you look amazing," Kane declared once he'd applied the lotion, stopped the cap of the bottle, and stood back to admire Eli. "And whoever said perfection can't be made more perfect, they've never seen you like this, that's without word of a lie."

Eli felt his cheeks warm; a common thing lately. "It feels kinda strange having my bits and pieces covered in this stuff, I've got to admit."

Kane chuckled. "It's important to look your best tonight."

"I understand."

And Eli did. A lot was riding on the success of the dinner.

"Now, you know what to do and what to say, don't you?" Kane added, somewhat nervously Eli believed, while turning his attention to the massive dining room table's centrepiece, an almost life-sized ice statue of Michelangelo's "David", one that'd been delivered not that long ago.

It was a good thing Eli didn't answer the door then; the delivery guys would have copped the sight of a real dick, not just a sculpted one in ice. And Eli was only prepared to show himself to his Master's guests, not some randos.

"I do," Eli answered, nodding.

At that, there was a knock on the door.

Eli's nerves turned for a bit within him. Kane,

obviously sensing this, reassured him with, "You will be magnificent and loved."

"Thank you."

He went to the door.

On opening it, he was greeted by three men in tidy and expensive looking business suits with tight expressions. That was until they feasted their eyes on Eli proper.

Before they could comment, positively or otherwise, Eli said, "Welcome to my Master's home. I'm his boy and I'm here to ensure you're looked after. May I take your coats, please?"

All three stood there, mouths agape and not moving.

Eli, loving that they found him so captivating.

More confidently, he repeated his greeting, adding, "And may I also ask what aperitif's you'd like? I can offer you a lovely vermouth, or a nice bubbly champagne, or even a tasty dry sherry from the drink's cabinet, gentlemen. Your choice. I'm here to serve you."

One of the men, the tallest and better looking of the three, mostly because he wasn't so portly, came to life. "You are the most handsome boy I've ever seen. Simply beautiful!"

The other two agreed with pleasant grunts.

The man then said, "And if this is how the evening has begun, Kane-san has done well. Very well indeed."

Eli offered a little bow. "I'm glad to hear that."

"As you should be," the man said, smiling now as his attention took all of Eli in. "But please, we are at your disposal, boy."

"Then please follow me, gentlemen."

From there, everything seemed rather dreamlike and pleasant. Eli attended to the three men, his Master too, and everyone, including himself, seemed to be enjoying themselves.

They also offered their compliments often. Eli liked that, lapped it up, in fact. But most of all, not one of them touched him with anything else but their admiring stares, just as Kane had promised.

"Thank you, sir," Eli offered when one of the men complimented him again.

He thanked them all often.

When the meal was done, the last course served, a cheese and wine deal, Kane sat up after wiping his mouth with his napkin. "Can you get the kibi dango I've made especially for this evening please, boy?"

"Yes, I can, Master."

More nods and agreeing comments.

The more handsome man said, "He is such an obedient and wonderful boy, Kane-san. You are most fortunate to have him."

Kane smugly replied, "Thank you, Ikon-san. He is not only obedient and wonderfully perfect as you can plainly see, he is greatly loved too. Loved so much it's with all of my heart, let me tell you all."

The largest man said, "If he's available after he's served you, I'd like to have him."

Kane's face darkened. "He won't be available—sorry to disappoint you, Takahashi-san."

Eli was relieved to hear those words.

"I can certainly understand that," Takahashi said, pressing his lips together. "I'd not want to let him go if he were mine, either. He is most delicious in every way."

"He will always be mine," Kane offered, smiling lovingly at Eli.

Eli liked how his Master made it clear what the boundaries were, more so because they were spoken in front of others and not just to him in private.

He couldn't help himself when he said, "I will always be yours, Master, for as long as you desire me." And with that he couldn't help but get aroused.

The guests certainly appreciated his sudden semi.

"I will always desire you, boy," Kane replied, patting Eli's buttocks, smiling wolfishly at the same time. "Always."

Eli went into the kitchen to fetch the platter of kibi dango with a smile on his lips and a song in his heart, knowing without doubt that he *would* let his Master masturbate him so he could season the dumplings for their guests.

Although as he retrieved the food from the larder, that's when he heard moaning again. Moaning that caused him to pause, for it sounded like whoever was making it was in pain.

Terrible pain.

Eli's heart raced. The door to the hallway that led to the cellar was closed. He couldn't open it, not without permission. His curiosity burned, but he had to get back into the dining room.

He'd ask Kane about the moaning later.

When he returned to the dining room carrying the kibi dango on an expensive looking silver platter, the guests and Kane were standing, talking lightly amongst themselves, nodding and smiling too. He heard his Master discuss how they should now retire to the more comfortable lounge room where they would enjoy a strong drink.

All agreed with him.

Eli, without being asked, said, "Master, I'd like it if you would masturbate me for our guest's pleasure so I can season these kibi dango for them."

The three men's mouths dropped open once more.

Before they recovered, Kane asked, "Are you sure, boy?"

"I am, Master."

"Then that's what will happen." Kane gestured for the guests to proceed to the loungeroom, brightening and beaming a smile. When the men had exited the dining room, Kane grabbed Eli, pulling him close to kiss his forehead. "Thank you, my heart."

"No problem."

From there, once more, everything remained dreamlike. More so because once he'd served the guests their glasses of more potent alcohol, scotch on the rocks mostly, he was soon on Kane's lap and wrapped in his love.

Eli was hard in seconds.

The men remained silent, watching intently, as Kane touched Eli to the point of making him writhe in ecstasy, moaning, mouth agape and dripping as much as his dick leaked.

From there, it didn't take long.

Mostly because Kane's words had meant so much to him, had spurred him on to fire his arousal unlike any other time. In fact, by the time he got that familiar feeling consuming him, right at the edge, Eli knew he was as horny as he'd ever been.

"I'm…going to c-cum, Master!" he cried with a shudder, all hot and intoxicated with Kane's presence, actions, and love.

The platter of kibi dango was produced in the nick of time. Because Eli, yelping and shuddering, stars scintillating in his vision, weak kneed and all, covered them with his love for his Master.

Seasoned them really well for his Master's guests too.

The kibi dango were then offered to amazed looks and to so much appreciation and many compliments as well. Eli was still too much in a confused post-orgasmic daze to take note of much else.

After a moment of anticipation as to what the guests would think, strangely nervous after cooling somewhat, Eli asked, "Did I do well?"

"You really did," Kane whispered into Eli's ear, before returning his attention to the others. "My boy has the most exquisite taste, doesn't he, gentlemen?" Eli then realized how exhilarating it had been because others watched him being pleasured by the man he loved. "And don't you think his ejaculate is the absolutely perfect seasoning to the kibi dango, even if I do say so myself."

The men all nodded in agreement, relishing what they'd been given to taste by expressing their gratitude.

Ikon said, "It certainly has the right tang to it, Kane-san. Not too bitter, either."

All agreed again.

"Thank you, Ikon-san. It didn't take much to get it that way either." Kane kissed Eli on his forehead after brushing his hair aside, showing his affection by keeping hold of him too. "He looks after himself."

"We can see that," one man sitting next to Ikon said.

"Yes, you're a very lucky man to have such a beautiful and fit boy," Ikon added chewing on a mouthful before swallowing his dumpling and licking his lips.

Kane once more thanked them.

Takahashi, the one who'd remained silent most of the night, only looking at Eli, staring like a hungry dog mostly, piped up. "You will have all the backing you need for your restaurant, Kane-san." He eyed Eli again, a smile crawling over his lips. "And you can thank your boy for giving us a perfect demonstration of your concept for this decision."

"Thank you, Takahashi-san." Kane kissed Eli again and again, that time on his lips; another thrill given with an audience that made his head go all lovely and giddy again. "He knows he's thanked, don't you, boy?"

"I do, Master."

More nods and approval from the three businessmen.

Ikon interjected, "I also agree with you, Takahashi-san. I too like the idea of having the waiters of the restaurant remain naked so they can then season your speciality dish at the guest's table for them when required."

The two others nodded.

Kane nodded too. "Yes, a good step up from the nantaimori experience I offered before. This will take things to a new level, one I'm sure my guests will very much enjoy."

"And open their wallets for," Takahashi supplied.

All agreed.

"I would pay good money for this—it's most delicious. A delicacy, even," Ikon interjected, sucking on his fingers after eating his seasoned kibi dango. "A lot of money."

Kane said, "I think it would be reasonable to charge a thousand dollars a head at least for such an experience, don't you?"

"If the waiters you hire are as beautiful as your boy, I'd charge double that," Takahashi said, leaning forward and smiling. "I'd also add an additional charge for the seasoning, especially if it's prepared at the table for the guests to witness."

The two others almost cheered at that.

"A good suggestion, Takahashi-san," Kane said, offering a bow of his head.

At that, Takahashi stood. "This evening has been most enjoyable; and as I said, you really do have your boy to thank for that, Kane-san. He was a true delight."

"I know I do, thank you, Takahashi-san," Kane replied, embracing Eli with even more love and intent. "And yes, he is a delight. A perfect one."

Eli didn't remember much after that.

He'd done what had been asked of him and more. He'd pleased his Master. Perhaps tonight after the guests have said their farewells, Kane would fuck him, the desire for that to happen more than overwhelming him already.

He could only hope, anyway.

He did remember Kane whispering into his ear as the last guest left, "I'm going to give you your reward to thank you for what you've done for me tonight. How does that sound, my heart?"

"It sounds wonderful."

The Fifth Day

1.5: Boy will not tamper with any keys or locks without Master's permission. Boy will not go into any room Master does not wish him to without explicit permission. Punishment will result if disobeyed on this matter.

Friday, 5:15 am

Eli was woken by a storm. He sat up, heart racing from the sudden flash of lightning followed by a boom of thunder that rattled the windowpanes fifteen seconds later. The count meant the storm was close, less than five kilometres.

Without thought, he snuggled next to Kane.

"Are you frightened?" Kane said bringing Eli into his hold.

"Not when I'm in your arms."

While he was held with love, caressed, and kissed, the storm came closer then passed quickly. By the time it was rumbling in the distance, Eli began to feel different urges.

"Can I suck your dick before we get up, Master?"

"You may, boy." Kane moved so he could untie his silken pyjamas, reveal his big, thick dick hard with morning glory. "And besides, a swallow of protein before breakfast will be good for you."

"I know it will be."

Eli eagerly moved his attention toward his goal. He grabbed it, feeling its heat, admiring its hardness within his hand like it was a reflection of his Master's strength.

"I love how you hold my cock so tightly, boy."

"And I love that I can have it, Master," Eli replied as he licked around the swollen knob, tasting his Master's salt, inhaling the manly pungency of him too. "I love it so much."

At that, Eli opened his mouth and did his best to take in as much of Kane's erection as he could. He sucked, slurped, and licked with all his enthusiasm, sometimes gagging, but always making sure to look up. That way Kane could see his eyes wet with his love and his mouth stuffed with his dick.

Kane must have appreciated that. "Such a beautiful sight."

Eli increased his attention by moving his hand in time with his deep throating. Kane quickly shuddered. A moan and writhe after that, Eli was given his reward, hot and thick into his mouth.

He swallowed, enjoying the tangy, somewhat salty bitterness that followed. The alkaline aftertaste too. It was no longer just one big dump of intense saltiness to him as he thought his own tasted like after eating the kibi dango. Perhaps his palate was already becoming used to such nuances of flavor.

Or was it because Kane's was a different taste?

Whatever the reason, Eli was soon hugged and kissed for what he'd done. Wonderfully so. And while he was held, wrapped so tightly within his safe place, his world now, he then noticed that his Master's dick hadn't deflated despite him recently cumming. Eli got another idea. One which he also yearned for now he thought about his own erection causing him to ache delightfully.

He whispered, "I need your dick in me now, please, Master."

Kane chuckled. "You're like the cricket who desires the ripened crops before harvest, aren't you, my heart?"

Eli, blushing, shy and unable to take his eyes off Kane, heat surrounding him, his own most of all, simply offered, "I love being with you."

"And as such you're always hungry for my attention, aren't you, boy?"

"Is there anything wrong with that, Master?"

"There isn't." He moved so he could look Eli in the eyes. "And I want to give you what you desire for all you've done for me lately, boy."

Eli's heart skipped a beat. "You're going to fuck me, then, Master?"

"I am."

Eli shivered; he was that delighted. "Thank you. Thank you so much, Master. I will do my best for you as I become a part of you again."

"I know you will."

"And what position would you like me in this time?"

"I want to fuck you from behind—it will be a different feeling for you, but I know you'll love it."

"I know I will."

And it was true. Eli felt different sensations as he was taken from behind, his prostate rubbed by the underside of his Master's cock to make it so this time. But most of all, in that position—head down, ass up—he felt the most submissive.

And that was a good thing.

More so when his Master grabbed him by his neck to turn his head so he could be kissed. Owned with Kane's tongue just as much as his dick.

Eli was in heaven once more.

What bliss.

When Kane came again, panting, sweating, and grabbing at Eli's hips, trembling while behind him, shuddering and yelling his joy, Eli came at the same time too; his cum squirted all over the sheets. Once his Master pulled out and got up off the bed, Eli turned around to face him.

He missed Kane so much.

More kisses were given equally.

When parted, still feeling the euphoria, Kane said, "Go clean yourself off while I make you your breakfast, my heart."

"I will." Eli smiled, so loved and warm inside him. "And thank you again, Master."

"You are most welcome, boy."

Jiro could already tell things were different. Not only was he not used as a sexual object today, his abuser sat farther down the bed than usual. He hadn't been drugged, either.

What had changed?

Was it Eli? Had something happened to him? Jiro

had to know, but at the same time he wouldn't give his abuser the satisfaction of knowing he was curious. He didn't want to give him any at all. None whatsoever.

As a result, the silence that hung between them like a bad smell was almost deafening. Jiro let the man stew. He wasn't giving him anything unless it was forcefully taken.

Which no doubt it would be…soon enough.

After a deep sigh that broke the uneasy quiet, his abuser simply said, "It's such a beautiful day after the storm this morning, isn't it?"

Jiro almost choked on his own tongue. "If by 'beautiful' you mean it is for someone who's not chained to a bed and sexually abused every day, then yeah, I suppose it fucking is. A fucking magnificent day too, no less."

His abuser snorted but didn't look at him. "Are you still complaining? It's growing tiresome, you know."

"Oh, I'm so sorry I'm inconveniencing you with my problems you caused, you fucking cunt!"

A pistol was produced from within the man's fancy jacket. "I could always end those problems."

Jiro's sudden gripping fear at the sight of the weapon struck him hard, twisting like a knife inside him as he tried to get as far away as possible from his abuser. He couldn't. His skin crawled, right to the back of his neck.

"I'm…s-sorry," was all he could manage through that blinding panic, unable to do anything but move his legs and shift himself to the wall to become even more cornered.

The man pointed the gun at him. "It's interesting that

with one squeeze of my finger, I can end your pathetic life, isn't it?" He stood, aiming it more carefully.

As Jiro gulped, he felt his bladder release, nowhere for his fear to go but all over himself. "I'm...really s-sorry. I won't...disrespect you...not ever a-again."

"You know," his abuser chuckled, cocking the weapon, "blood and bone makes for a great fertilizer. Imagine your ground up remains scattered all over the dirt where my flowers grow within my private gardens and how useful you'll become to me then. A far better thing to be than the wretched cowering boy I see before me now."

Jiro felt his hot tears fall, unable to help himself. "You...I have no w-way to convince you...to not pull the t-trigger, have I?"

A shrug. "Also imagine, and this is the most delightful part, how within those private gardens I'll be fucking your brother knowing your body is scattered around him while he screams for more of my cock. And scream for it he does. He simply hungers for my love all the time now, it's quite embarrassing, really."

Jiro blubbered, "I can't...s-stop you." The tears fell even more. "If you're g-going to...do it...*do it*."

"Are you giving me your permission to kill you?" A pause. A cruel smile. "And just so you know, this time I'm more than happy to oblige. I don't need you anymore and you've served your purpose." A snort that time. "And besides, Eli pleases me more than you ever did. You failed, Jiro."

"I'm...sorry."

"You will be—and just so you know, my name is

Kane. Kane Nakamori." A cruel smile as a silencer was slowly screwed onto the end of the pistol. "So goodbye, Jiro. It was fun while it lasted."

Jiro could only see the end of the gun now as everything else around him fell into darkness because of his debilitating fear. This was it. He couldn't save Eli.

He really had failed.

Friday, 4:23 pm
Kane had been gone for hours.

Something that'd been prepared for because his Master's last words before he left were, "If I find out you haven't done as I've told you today, I'll fit a chain onto your collar and then tie you to the bedpost for the night as punishment. Understand me, boy?"

Eli gulped. "I understand, Master."

He didn't like the sound of that, more so because his Master seemed serious. Deadly serious. He also looked distant and kind of sad as well.

What was going on?

As Eli wondered, he was kissed on his forehead. "But if you do as I've asked, today most of all, your rewards will be many. That much I can promise you."

"I won't disappoint you."

"I know you won't."

And while Eli had been given permission to make his own lunch—so long as it was healthy—he couldn't help but ponder Kane's moody behavior which resulted in his long absence.

He missed Kane so much.

After he'd eaten his tuna salad sandwich, deciding to do so in the kitchen, he realized how quiet the large house was without Kane. Eerily so. He didn't like it. Not at all.

After cleaning up the dishes and completing the rest of his daily chores quickly, Eli found that something wasn't right. Didn't feel right, either.

He didn't know why.

Eli turned his attention to the door beyond the larder that led down to the cellar. It was open. He went to it, swallowing hard and feeling nervous for no reason he understood. What was that about?

The hallway beyond was dark, so he flicked on the light.

The first thing confronting Eli was the fact the rug that'd been placed down by Kane to help him with his phobia of joins between tiling had been moved, now scrunched up at the end of the hall nearer the cellar's door.

This puzzled him.

Why would it be like that?

To make matters worse, the way to the door to the right, the one where he believed he'd heard the moaning sounds coming from for the last few days, was hindered by the exposed mosaic.

He looked down at them—there were scuff marks. Had they always been there, or were they fresh? Had something been removed from the locked room recently, because now that he thought about it, he hadn't noticed those marks before.

Eli, without even realizing it, soon found himself at that door, holding its handle but looking down to see his bare feet unmistakably on the tiny tiles and the myriad of joins between them.

He blinked.

A moment of nothing.

More blinking, still feeling nothing.

"That's…strange," he said to himself.

And it was. Because for the first time in a long time—since that fateful day anyway—he didn't break out in a cold sweat because of his fears. Didn't feel the urge to run away. Not even the need to seek help, like an embrace from anyone—Kane's most of all.

He harrumphed while he gripped the handle. During which time, Eli, profoundly so, realized one very important thing right then. Kane's love and his love for Kane in return, had helped ease some of his anxiety. He no longer felt burdened by it.

Not this particular aspect of his phobia, anyway.

Eli smiled.

"He's done this to me. He's been repairing me without me even realizing it." His love for Kane then couldn't be more profound.

His hand hovered for a moment before he withdrew it. "I'm not going to disobey my Master." And with that, he trotted off toward the lounge room where he was told to wait for Kane's return after he'd done his chores.

While he waited, Eli thought about all the pleasure he'd get because he'd been a good boy for his Master.

Friday, 5:21 pm
Kane finally returned, thank God.

"Welcome home, Master!" Eli blurted with joy, jumping up and rushing into open arms where he was loved and where he belonged.

"Thank you, my heart." Kane held him tighter, Eli believing he held back emotions, as he sniffled often. He had missed Eli too. "It's so good to be back."

"I've done everything you've told me to do today."

"Good boy. Then lie down, I'm going to fuck you until you cum for me!"

"Oh, yes, Master! Thank you!"

Friday, 7:15 pm

The dinner Kane prepared was exquisite: shoyu ramen with chicken. It was one of Eli's favorite meals made even more delicious because it was so tasty. When eaten, his Master feeding it to him as he fed Eli all his meals, they sat together on the couch in front of the TV. They watched a Samurai movie again; this time the classic *Seven Samurai*. Eli admitted he liked these types of movies, especially all the code of honor stuff.

"Did you fancy a drink, boy?" Kane asked when the first film was done.

"What kind of drink, Master?"

Kane kissed Eli's forehead. "I think a celebration is in order. How about fetching a bottle of Moët? Yes, that would do nicely, don't you think?"

"What's the occasion? Didn't we celebrate your deal being closed last night?"

"We did." Kane sat up. "But do I need an excuse to celebrate with my boy?"

"No, of course not, Master."

"Good. Then go get the bottle from the cellar for me, please." Kane smiled, one warm and beautiful. "You also have my permission to open any doors you'll need to do this task for me, boy."

Eli stood. "Then I'll be right back, Master, so we can celebrate our love for each other again and again."

"A very good reason to do so, indeed." But Eli swore he saw a flash of sadness cross his Master's expression then.

With a new kind of worry finding him, he had to ask, "Are you all right, Master?"

A breath in and a glinting-eyed look. A smile, one Eli believed was thoughtful even if still enigmatic. A sadness behind it all though. "I am because of you, my heart."

Eli leaned down to kiss Kane. "Then I am too because of you."

The kiss shared became profound, deep and as loving as Eli had ever experienced. He shuddered with delight because of it. Got all giddy and weak-kneed too.

But most of all he got hard.

When he parted, he giggled. "Now look what you did to me."

Kane ran his long fingers over the length of Eli's throbbing shaft, ending at his foreskin where he rubbed it gently to stimulate him even more. Eli felt hot flushes course through him too. He loved his Master's sensual attention most of all.

"When you return with the bottle of Moët, I'll help you out with that too, boy."

"I can't wait, Master."

"Neither can I."

Eli dashed away, heart racing with his love, his hard-on waggling, slapping against him, too, to leave little wet spots on either side of his hips. He couldn't wait to be fucked again. But as he left the lounge room proper, there was a loud knock on the front door, startling him.

"Answer the door for me, will you, boy?"

Eli knew he had to obey, but at the same time didn't want whoever was calling at this hour to see his nakedness. For a brief moment, he was in a quandary. That was until he thought about his unconditional and undying love for Kane. Love he knew without doubt was returned.

"Yes, Master," was the only answer Eli knew he could give, solving the minor problem even if his cheeks burned with embarrassment.

His erection had deflated too, sadly so. Eli hoped the visitor wasn't going to stay too long.

He opened the front door.

The early evening beyond was crisp and clear, the fading sunlight staining the cloudless sky beautiful oranges and yellows. Birds twittered, their final calls before roosting. If it were warmer, Eli would have loved to have spent the rest of the night in the private garden off the main bedroom with Kane.

A man cleared his throat.

Eli remembered the reason for opening the door. To his surprise, it was the chauffeur standing there looking worried and a little flustered—if Eli was reading things right.

"Is your Master home?" the man asked politely.

"He is, yes."

A moment of thought, a change of tone too. "Then get to fetching him, boy."

Eli didn't like the man's change in attitude. "Why?"

The chauffeur shrugged. "Makes no difference to me, but I was about to put the car in for the night when I found something terrible, didn't I."

"What did you find?" Eli was more than curious if such a discovery warranted the man to come knocking on the door.

The chauffeur never came to the house.

"A body," the man replied matter-of-factly. "I found a body over by the potting shed. Most terrible, it is. The poor man was shot in the head right between the eyes."

Eli was stunned.

Without further thought, he blurted, "Take me to him."

"You're all starkers, you are—you'll catch a death of cold out here, if not worse."

"I don't care."

"Well, I do." A huff was offered. "I've seen enough naked men to last me a lifetime tonight. Might be Master's thing to like your sort, but it ain't mine, that's for sure."

"What are you insinuating?"

"The man who's been shot is all starkers too."

That wasn't what Eli meant, but before he could relay his thoughts, mostly because he believed "your sort" was a dig at him being gay, from behind him Kane grabbed Eli's hand to hold it.

Eli turned to his Master, relieved he was here.

Really relieved.

"What's going on here, Jason?" Kane ordered. "Explain yourself, and why you felt the need to interrupt my evening."

The man seemed to shrink. "As I was saying to your boy here, I found a body."

"Where?" Kane barked, not impressed at all if Eli was reading things right.

The chauffeur bowed. "Follow me, sir."

Eli, Kane's hand still within his, wonderfully so, went out into the evening to follow the chauffeur. If circumstances were different, he would have enjoyed the walk with his Master.

It would have been romantic.

Unfortunately, the circumstances were far worse when the potting shed came into sight, the structure of it nestled within thick gardens lovingly tended to.

Eli's world came crashing in around him as he realized one thing to his absolute debilitating, numbing, horror as he approached the scene. As things came into focus. The body wasn't just anyone.

It was his brother.

HIS BROTHER!

"Jiro!" Eli wailed as he felt all his strength seep out of him, drain him to his soul, and he collapsed next to his older brother in a heap of rising grief. "Oh God! Jiro. Noooo!"

And as the tears fell, shoulders shuddering, hiccupping now, Eli brought his beautiful brother into his arms, his hands and body shaking uncontrollably with sorrow.

"Nooo, Jiro! Noooo!"

Kane knelt next to him, holding Eli around his shoulder. "I'm so sorry this has happened to him, but I feel this is all my fault, my heart," he whispered, his voice also thick with his emotions.

Eli, after letting those words sink in through his pain, replied, "H-how is this…your f-fault?"

"Today I tried to get Yukkon to let Jiro go to try and surprise you." Kane paused; his eyes watery. "And this was the result of my request."

Eli wiped his face wettened with his sorrow, lips trembling, his heart worse; it was broken. "Then…then we've g-got to let the…cops k-know about this—Mason's fiancé is a c-cop. I'll call…him."

Kane brushed his hand over Eli's cheek gently before kissing away some of the flowing tears. "If you do that, I'll be the next body you'll have to cradle in your arms."

"Wh-what are y-you saying?" Eli began to shiver all over, and not from the cool weather—the piece now missing from him took away so much, including his warmth.

Kane softly replied, "I'm now a marked man because of what I did for you."

"No! Nooo!" Eli couldn't believe how his safe and beautiful world full of so much love had been turned around so quickly. "You c-can't be. No! You…can't. Nooo! this c-can't be…can't be happening."

Kane lowered his head. "It is, I'm afraid."

Eli, holding Jiro, found he was soon held by Kane at the same time. Taken lovingly into his safe place, even though the horror and grief around him pervaded his every thought and emotion.

He cried and cried in Kane's arms for God knows how long, let it all out, time holding no meaning as he did. How could it? Jiro was dead. His beautiful brother had been murdered in cold blood.

Murdered.

Murdered by Yukkon.

Murdered all because of what? Eli didn't even know, other than one day he got that package with Jiro's severed finger and ring along with a note about how he had to wait for further instructions. From there Mason called his Uncle Joe and a while later Kane showed up; Eli never got the further demands. And that's what made it even worse. There was no reason for what had happened. None at all.

"I'll make sure his body is treated with respect and buried with the honor he deserves, my heart. We will have a private funeral for him to respect his life and to offer our farewells."

Eli nodded within Kane's hold. "Thank y-you."

"Anything for you, my heart."

Eli looked up at that moment, his emotion-soaked eyes meaning everything was blurry, awfully so. "I don't k-know what I'd do…what I'd do w-without you, Kane."

"I don't know what I'd do without you, either." And

with that, Kane kissed Eli upon his trembling wet lips, soft and beautiful and so full of love, Eli's broken heart fluttered.

They both cried together after that.

The Last Day

1.6: When Boy is released from his contract, he is no longer Master's property. He is no longer at Master's whims. He is no longer an object for sexual gratification. He is a free boy.

Unknown day, 9:05 am

Eli had cried within Kane's arms for God knows how long before the funeral. When exactly it happened, he didn't know; it could have been the day after or a couple of days. He was too grief-stricken to count days any longer. And what meaning did time hold now that his brother, his only family, was no longer with him? None. None whatsoever.

Eli cried and cried.

The funeral was a deeply sad ceremony held within the large garden conservatory of the house: only Kane, Eli, and a minister in attendance. After Kane had asked, the casket was a closed one on Eli's request. He couldn't bear to see Jiro's dead body again. That terrible image of him lying in the dirt, naked and so cold, would give him nightmares for the rest of his life as it was.

He didn't need that added too.

Also, Kane allowed Eli to wear clothing for the day of the funeral, something he appreciated, for sure. Although, once he was back in the house and within the safety of Kane's arms, he shed them. Being naked for his Master was a symbol of his love, he realized—exposed and raw and beautiful.

"I really don't deserve you, my heart," Kane said, bringing Eli into his arms, holding him.

"You do…and I love you for that."

"I love you too."

From then, Eli was warmly kissed and lovingly cared for. Really cared for. Kane did everything for him, not leaving him for one moment.

Not one.

He really appreciated that as well.

On the morning of whatever day that it so happened to be, Kane said, "I will bath you now, my heart."

"Will you…umm, make me my breakfast after that?" Eli wiped away his tears for a moment after he'd been thinking of Jiro, knowing without doubt there would be more following soon.

"Of course, I will." Kane ran his gentle touch over Eli's back. "Let me keep doing everything for you, my heart. It pleases me so much to do so."

"Thank you—and as I said, I don't know what I'd do without you."

"I feel the same."

Not that Eli ate much—a mere few mouthfuls—when breakfast was served inside the bedroom this morning, even though the food was tasty and perfectly cooked, as always. His broken heart was all that consumed him now.

He only wanted Jiro back.

So much so, it now hurt him beyond any pain he'd

ever felt in all his life; the worst part of it all was knowing that he'd never see his brother again.

Eli still felt weak with grief.

As Kane helped him up, Eli noticed a man, white-haired and wearing overalls, in the private garden beyond the voile wafting in the breeze because the French doors were open to the air this morning. The day was warm and crisp already.

"Who's that?" he felt compelled to ask.

Kane replied, "He is my gardener. But ignore him please; he's just spreading some blood and bone over the soil to help the flowers grow as beautiful as you are, that's all."

"Right..." Eli returned his attention to who mattered. "Kiss me."

"With pleasure." Kane did so. "Perhaps after I've washed you, we can be together in the private garden that's just been fertilized."

"I'd love that."

"So would I, my heart."

Unknown day, 10:15 am

After Eli stepped out of the bath, Kane dried him. "You know, sitting in all that hot water has really made me want to pee, big time," he said truthfully.

Kane smiled, no longer enigmatically but lovingly and with sadness in his eyes. Was he sad because Eli was grieving...or was it something else? Something deeper?

"Ah, so it *wasn't* those two glasses of freshly squeezed

orange juice you drank at breakfast then, boy?" he questioned lightly.

Eli managed to return the smile; the first time his expression had lightened since...well, he didn't want to keep thinking about that. "I think you might be right there, Master."

Kane was gently dabbing Eli's reddened skin with a soft towel. "When you do go, I'll hold it for you."

"Oh...all right."

It was an experience, kind of "exposing" really, to have someone hold his dick while he tried to piss. No lie. And yes, Eli was used to being naked all the time now, so that was saying something.

This had taken all of that to a new level.

"Do you pull back your foreskin when you go?" Kane asked before the flow came—Eli, kind of getting stage fright, was deep in his feelings about what was happening.

"I...just a little bit, yes."

"Good." Kane did so gently. "You can go now, boy."

"Yes, Master."

And he did go.

Kane had aimed it so Eli's stream went into the toilet's bowl, the sound of it doing so filling his ears moments later. All the while, his Master's breathing was felt in his ear as he was held tightly with his other arm.

Things started to get warmer between them.

As expected, Eli felt his crawling lust rise up within him by the time he'd finished answering nature's call, his dick engorging to a proud semi. From there, to full erection, achingly so.

"I think it's time I took you into the private garden," Kane whispered.

"Where you'll be fucking me, I hope."

"Most definitely."

The morning had turned even warmer, almost to a humid stickiness—perhaps another storm was brewing. This time of year, it wasn't unheard of to have such changes in weather.

Eli was led, hand in hand, into the place where his heart belonged. Because within their private garden, with Kane becoming an intimate part of him, that's where he felt the most at peace. That's when his worries and everything else that burdened him dissipated for a brief, wonderful moment.

All thanks to Kane.

To complete the picture of sanctuary and serenity, butterflies fluttered lazily around the flowers, now in full bloom, greeting the sunshine. Eli was laid down onto the daybed.

"I don't deserve you, truly I don't," Kane said as he began his journey of tender and gentle kisses all over Eli's body.

"I don't deserve you, either," Eli admitted.

"You do. You deserve all the love anyone can give you."

"Then I have what I need, because your love satisfies me. How can it not? You do everything for me, even the things I didn't know I needed you to do."

Kane was paying attention to Eli's hard-on, licking

and kissing it, sending delightful tingles all through him. "I must do the honorable thing," he said barely audibly.

And then the strangest thing happened. Kane began to cry. It wasn't an outpouring of emotions like a dam had been breached, but a gentle trickle as his eyes became wetter and tears fell from his lashes.

Eli sat up onto his elbows. "Are you all right, Master?"

"I'm perfectly all right." Kane's finger was paying attention to Eli's ass now, preparing it. More shivers of carnal pleasure the result. "You are the most beautiful and precious boy I've even known. You deserve so much, even more than what I can give you."

"Don't talk like that," Eli's worry soon found him again even though his body raged with his yearning for his Master. "You give me *more* than enough."

Kane's tears continued to fall. "You say that, but I know I can do more for you…so much more, my heart."

"Then how about you just fuck me?" Eli growled, feeling the urges begin to overwhelm him and overtake everything else once more. "That's the *more* from you I need right now. Truly!"

A smile with wettened lips, both from his tears and his attention upon Eli's dick. "With pleasure."

From there, the both of them became one. Kane took Eli into his arms while moving his hips, thrusting and gaining rhythm while Eli moaned, writhed and shuddered underneath his Master.

They didn't just fuck that time…they created an even greater bond between them.

And if Eli didn't know any better, he'd say that right

now, at this time, he'd never felt so connected to Kane. His Master had never been like this before, so passionate while he trembled with his emotions, all of it coming to the fore as even more tears flowed. Eli not only felt his heated body, but tasted his sadness too. Something was certainly different.

Very different.

"I don't deserve you, boy," Kane whispered while shuddering, Eli knowing he'd cum inside him.

Eli was close himself. "You keep saying that, Master."

"It's because I must, it's the truth."

Eli was confused. Although he really didn't have the power of concentration to wonder why, Kane's dick, hard as ever, was still inside him even though the man had reached his climax—Eli coming to his now, too, with great overwhelming quivers and moans reflecting his visceral delights.

They remained holding each other for an eternity, close and wonderful, sharing breaths, looks, and knowing smiles as much as their love. Eli couldn't help feel emotional about it all himself, and also felt his eyes sting. Kane kissed him and kissed him.

They kissed each other for another eternity.

When parted, breathless, and tingling all over, Eli said, "You're...staying inside me?" He kept up with his moaning when Kane began thrusting once more.

Already Eli's prostate was amazingly stimulated, but because of Kane's continuation, he quickly felt that deep buzz inside him, causing his post-orgasmic state to heighten.

His thoughts became all muddled as well, even more so.

Such bliss.

Kane must have felt the same while he held Eli and Eli held him with as much intent in return, his Master's tears still falling as more salted kisses were given.

On parting again, Kane said, "I want to be with you for as long as I can be, that's why I'm staying inside you."

"You...you make it sound like you're leaving."

Kane offered even more kisses, so overwhelming to be kissed and worshipped so much, all over Eli's lips, cheeks, and ears. "I will always be with you, my heart. No matter what."

"I don't want you to leave me."

"I won't."

Kane came again, grunting loudly, shuddering unbelievably, as he delivered his cum deep into Eli's guts. From there, he collapsed and held Eli even tighter.

They held each other for another span of forever, it seemed.

When parted, sweaty, still heated, both from each other and the sunlight, Kane reached over and picked up something from off the table they ate at often.

"This is for you, my heart," he said handing Eli an envelope.

Eli, his thoughts and body still in his second orgasm rush, as well as still feeling the tremors from the first, mumbled though quivering, almost unmoving lips. "You... you're asking m-me to read something...while you're... you're still inside m-me?"

Kane nodded, brushing his touch over Eli's cheek. "I'm going to fuck you again while you do, too."

Eli sucked in a breath, unbelieving what he'd heard. "So soon?"

More smiles and tears. "Just read what I have done for you while I begin to work myself up again, boy."

"Yes, Master."

And from there, while Eli was fucked, every fibre of his being consumed by his Master's actions, his love, he tried his best to focus on the pages he'd pulled out of the envelope.

His eyes took a while to focus.

What he read astounded him as much as Kane going three times, kissing him more and more, Eli's eyes widening with each passing moment. Widening as much as the love he felt for Kane.

"I can't...accept this." Eli finally said as Kane came again, louder grunts to yelling the result of it.

That time Kane really did collapse onto Eli, pressed all his weight upon him, clearly spent. He was sweating profusely, his musk overtaking everything. Eli loved the smell of him. Loved Kane even more.

"You *will* accept it, my heart," his Master said, knocking him from his reverie. "It's my wish that you do so."

"But..." Eli had to take a moment as he re-read a lot of it now that Kane wasn't thrusting and groaning while above him; although his Master still remained inside even though he was now going flaccid. "But according to this...

you've given me your house and…and the restaurant…and all of your money."

Kane nodded. "If I die, you'll have everything I own."

"I *can't* accept that." Eli blurted, wondering why this had happened. What brought such a thing about? Eli didn't like how things had turned this morning from such encompassing beauty, loved multiple times to the point of exhaustion, to this.

"You can and you will—I don't want you left with nothing."

Eli then understood. "Yukkon…he's—please don't tell me what I think you're going to tell me."

Kane gave more kisses. "I told you that because of what I did for you, I'm now a marked man. It might happen today…it might happen tomorrow…but it will happen."

Eli's emotions bubbled up once more and he began to cry.

Kane held him.

For the longest time, that's how they remained, holding each other within their private garden drenched in nature's glory and their love. So much love.

After a while, Eli said, "But you're doing your best to protect yourself, aren't you?"

"I am, don't worry."

"You know I worry about you."

Kane brushed his fingers gently over Eli's lips. "As I worry about you."

Another thought then struck Eli, one that rose to the churning surface of all the others. "Can I ask you about something that's been bothering me, Master?" Eli leaned over, placing the paperwork onto the table, worry finding him for no other reason than it could again.

"You know you don't have to ask permission to do so. Ask away."

Eli paused, framing the next question in his mind as carefully as he could. "Over the past week, I've been hearing moaning coming from that locked room next to the kitchen. And...and the other day, when we found...Jiro, it looked like something had been dragged out of there."

"What are you saying, my heart?"

"I don't...know." And Eli didn't. "But...but did you succeed in rescuing Jiro...and then tried to do your best to help him? And you couldn't do much to save him because the bullet wound...was too great."

"No." Kane said matter-of-factly. "Jiro was shot at a close range from the look of the wound. He would have died instantly."

"Oh...okay."

Kane moved to look Eli deep into his eyes. "But just to put your mind at ease, that room holds the boiler and the excess supplies I use on the garden, sacks of fertilizer and the like."

"I see."

"The gardener needed a bag of fertilizer and I got it for him. You can go into the room and look for yourself, if you wish."

Eli believed Kane. "It's okay. I won't need to do that."

"You believe me?"

"With everything I am."

"Perfect." The enigmatic smile returned.

Unknown day, 1:32 pm

Eli remained in Kane's arms, safe and warm and once more loved hard before his Master got up off him, glistening with sweat, breathing heavily. He was so sexy, his dick dripping to emphasize all that had happened over the past few hours that delighted Eli to no end.

"I'm hungry," Kane announced. "Famished, to tell the truth."

Eli giggled. "I'm not surprised."

"You came as many times as I did, my heart."

"Only because you fucked it out of me." More laughter found Eli's lips—a nice feeling.

Kane joined in. "Would you like to make lunch for us today? Something simple—I fancy scrambled eggs on French toast."

Eli sat up, loving how he felt sore between his legs when he moved in such a way. Loved even more how he felt Kane's cum leaking out of him. "I'd be happy to make our lunch."

"Good boy. I appreciate this, as I hate to admit it but I'm exhausted and need to sit down for a moment."

"Again, I'm not surprised." Eli, also standing, kissed Kane that time. "I'll be right back."

"I look forward to it."

When Eli had left the beauty of the private garden, he realized he'd have to stop off at the toilet before he did anything else. He needed to clean himself. Because even though he wished he had a butt plug so he could keep Kane's cum inside him where it belonged, having it running down his inside leg meant he was left with no choice.

When done, he made his way to the kitchen.

With a realization that his heart was singing, the happiest he'd been since that terrible day when they found Jiro, Eli contemplated whether or not he should check the room that'd always been locked.

He shook his head, dismissing that thought.

"I trust him with my life, my handsome man named Kane."

After that, Eli got on with what he was asked to do. Soon, two plates of what Kane had desired to eat were ready. Eli trotted back toward the private garden where his Master, his love, his desire, and his safe place would be waiting.

"Master, your lun—"

At the sight of Kane, Eli dropped the food as a stunned disbelieving blanket, suffocating and unreal, fell over him. In a heartbeat, he fell to his knees, knowing all too well, terribly so, what had happened.

"Nooooo!" Eli managed as everything spinned.

The sight of Kane, his love, his Master, the only one who mattered in his life now, sitting back in his chair, lifeless, a bloom of blood over his chest, could only mean one thing.

He'd been shot.

Eli, fell onto his hands and knees before the grass hit him and he sunk into unconscious darkness, overwhelmed with an even greater grief than he could have ever imagined.

The New Day

1.7: When boy knows how to serve, he can be Master.

Two weeks later, Tuesday, 9:05 am
After a fortnight of counselling, enough tears to fill jars, and sadness that gripped him so much he couldn't move at times, a change happened within Eli. A newfound strength found him.

Kane's strength.

"I'm ready," he announced to Mason and Thomy; the two of them had been the ones who'd found Eli passed out in the garden, because through some miracle, a message to come to the house had been sent to them.

Kane must have sent it in his dying moments.

But Eli didn't want to think about the past anymore. It had done its damage and it had almost conquered him.

"You're going to…you know…run the restaurant, then?" Thomy asked.

"I am." Determination steeled even more within Eli. "In honor of not only Kane's memory, but Jiro's as well. I'm going to do my very best…for them."

"All right. In that case, is there anything I can do, Eli?"

"Yes…" Eli paused, moving to hold Thomy's hand.

"If you want to be the head waiter as we discussed earlier, I'd appreciate that."

Thomy's expression turned to surprise. "You mean…you want me to serve guests all naked and stuff?"

Eli nodded. "Only if you want to."

Thomy shrugged. "Maybe I *can* do that."

"Thank you—and I really do appreciate this, truly."

"Anything for you, Eli." A pause from Thomy. "But I don't wanna spackle all over folks' food. I'll leave that to the other guys you hire, if that's okay with you?"

"It's okay." Eli nodded. "And as the head waiter, you'll get to choose who does what. So up to you."

Thomy breathed relief. "Cool."

Mason came into Eli's view. "Are you still thinking about offering…what were they called?…kibi dango eaten from guy's asses as well?"

Eli replied quickly, "I am—it's what Kane would have wanted."

Mason didn't look too comfortable as he shot Thomy a look before returning his attention to Eli. "How do you even get past the food hygiene rules for something like that?"

Eli felt anger stab at him. "It's what I want to do. And what does it matter to you, Mason? It's *my* restaurant. Okay?"

Mason raised his hands in supplication. "Sorry…you're right."

Eli breathed, realizing he was holding his breath. "Are you still with me, Thomy?"

"I am, Eli. I am."

"I appreciate it," Eli returned.

"I'll always be there for you, Eli."

Eli turned to look at him, really glare, as once again strong feelings found him. He clenched his fists. "Don't say that—you don't know what it means. I do. And I don't want you to make promises to me you might not be able to keep."

Thomy seemed taken aback to the point of almost stepping back; his expression certainly deflated nevertheless. Eli liked that he was. It seemed the guy was submissive. That was good. "Sorry. I just meant I'd like to return the favor for you giving me a job that pays me like I'm a king. I mean, hell no, I ain't passing up on two-hundred and fifty bucks an hour to serve folks while I flash 'em me dick, that's for sure."

"That's good to hear." Eli sighed, relaxing. "Can you make me a cup of coffee, please, Thomy. You make the best coffees."

"Sure." At that, Thomy brushed his hand across Eli's, deliberately or not, Eli wasn't sure.

He kind of liked that Thomy did, though.

Quickly, Mason came to embrace Eli; his hugs never felt the same after Kane's all-enveloping love, but he appreciated it, nonetheless. "Hank told me the results of the autopsy...if you're interested, Eli."

"What difference would it make, Mason? He's dead—Yukkon murdered him and my brother. What more would I need to know?"

"Well...umm, a lot actually." Mason cleared his

throat. "Kane…he was shot in the heart, so he had about ten seconds to throw away the pis—"

"Stop!" Eli moved away from Mason. "I don't want to know. I want to remember the man I loved with all my heart through my time with him while he was alive. While I was his world and I was loved unlike at any other time before, ever. Is that too much to ask?"

Mason stared for a moment. "No…it's not."

Eli breathed, realizing he was holding his breath. "Thank you for being here for me lately, Mason." A deep breath. "Now, let's talk about the flowers I want to order regularly for the restaurant."

Mason's lips crawled to a smile. "I still can't believe you own a restaurant."

"I'd rather own it with my Kane…but yeah, I want to do it now more than ever."

"Thomy is looking forward to it—and I'm sure he'll do whatever you want him to, as well."

"He wants me to do anything I want to him lately, that's for sure." Eli nodded. "He's my boy, and I'm going to fuck him as much as I can. Perhaps even come to love him because I certainly know he has feelings for me."

Mason pulled away from Eli. "Um…what?"

Eli found he was smiling, even as he fingered his collar—one he'd never remove because it was the symbol of his Master's unbroken love for him. Love that could never be taken away, he realized, even now when he'd found someone else. Someone needy and vulnerable, as he'd been when Kane took him in under his care. "Thomy agreed to be my boy only yesterday."

"And…you've done it already?"

"We have."

Mason's expression softened. "All good then, I suppose."

"I suppose."

They both laughed.

Mason, breaking their embrace, was about to turn away and leave Eli's apartment, leave him with Thomy—who now lived with Eli but didn't want to mention it out loud—when he said, "Oh, I'm just checking here, but have you heard of Lima Syndrome? Because I know that's what saved you, Eli. I really do."

"No! What's that, then?" Eli didn't know what Mason was talking about, and not only did he feel a flash of annoyance course through him because of it again, he was confused most of all. "What are you talking about?"

"Never mind." Mason smiled along with his wave goodbye. "I'll talk to you later, buddy. Love you."

Eli relaxed. "I love you too, Mason."

But he relaxed too soon—Mason wasn't done.

Clearly.

His best friend cocked an eyebrow. "By the way, I forgot to tell you, Eli. Yukkon was found dead two weeks ago, too. He was shot and left for dead, just how you described how Jiro was left when you found him."

"That's the best news I've heard all day," Eli admitted, because it was.

Yukkon deserved to die after what he'd done.

Mason added, "Yeah…by the same gun that was used to kill Kane. Funny that, isn't it?"

Eli narrowed his stare at Mason. "What are you trying to say?"

Mason shrugged. "Nothing, I suppose. Just telling you." And with that he left, closing the door quietly.

When he'd done so, Thomy approached holding two coffees. "Here you are, Eli, get this down ya."

Eli took the cup, the coffee smelling wonderful. "Call me Master, Thomy, and I'll call you 'boy' from now on. It's what I want. All right?"

Thomy opened his mouth, closed it, then said, "Yes...Master."

"I'll also want you to sign a contract for me—I'll go get it, as I've prepared it already."

"Yes, Master."

The End

Author's Note

A Dom/sub contract should never be signed under duress, coercion, or blackmail. It is simply a more formal agreement between two people who desire a more respectful D/s dynamic, and may or may not have anything to do with romance or love. The contract will also state clear boundaries, definitions, and expectations for the both of them.

Lima Syndrome is the opposite of Stockholm Syndrome; it's where an abuser/captor falls in love or has affection/sympathy for their victim. In Eli's case, Kane fell so in love with him it was that love which saved him from Jiro's fate in the end.

Of course, Kane's blanketing love blinded vulnerable Eli too.

About the Author

By day I'm a humble physical therapist…and by day I'm also a writer of sweet & saucy boyslove stories (18+). I sleep at night as an old fart like me should. I'm both self-published and traditionally published. Other than that, I live with my partner and two cats and live my best life.

Website: http://konblackeboyslovewriter.com

Twitter: http://www.twitter.com/blackekon

Also by Kon Blacke
Published by Dreamsphere Books

Immortal Whispers
Kon Blacke

The Whispering Monks have foretold change to the world, and it's fast approaching. They also speak of the mortals who'll be involved.

Hereward, a lord knight who only worships the steel at his side, as the mad magician Ealdræd has taken away everyone he had ever loved. Wymond, an oblate determined to find his true self, even if it means turning away from everything he has ever known. Beornræd, a powerful magician who fears to love again after the cruelties of his past. Kieron, a stable hand with dragon blood flowing through his veins and is the rightful heir to a realm of unimaginable beauty.

All four will travel their own paths, to destroy their pasts and rebuild their future, as they thwart the evil plans of Ealdræd and his conduit, the immortal Abbot Hosho.

The whisperings continue through epic battles, both on the ground and in the sky.

The whisperings shall continue beyond the aftermath.

As it has been foretold.

More from Deep Desires Press

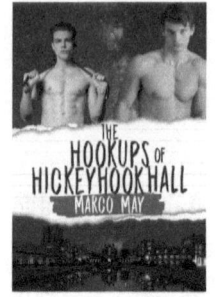

The Hookups of Hickeyhook Hall
Marco May

Jenner is gay and has a crush on Michael. Unbeknownst to him, Michael is bi and has a crush on him in return. But there's one huge obstacle in the way of professing his love. Their parents just got married to each other. Now, they're officially stepbrothers.

Both young men are determined to move on and leave their feelings behind, and what better way to do that than to dive into the challenges of starting a new life at Hickeyhook College? Their new lives are full of quirky roommates and stupid rules...and the discovery of an underground sex club with both students and staff that offers students the opportunity to cheat their way through to graduation without all the stresses of normal college life. With both young men in the club, it brings Jenner and Michael dangerously close, making it impossible to ignore the feelings they both swore to leave behind.

As sticky as their new situation is, it's about to get stickier. The powerful Dean Wicket sees the emerging relationship between Jenner and Michael and he's determined to get in the way...because he wants Michael to himself.

When the truth of Jenner and Michael comes out and the world is against them, these two men must fight with all they have to hold onto true love.

www.ingramcontent.com/pod-product-compliance
Lightning Source LLC
Chambersburg PA
CBHW022029170626
46808CB00003B/1111